Say Yes

Rob Ryder

Ryder Books
Ojai, California
www.ryderotica.com

Cover and Interior Design: Steven W. Booth
(And this guy is every writer's best friend.)
www.GeniusBookServices.com

Cover photographs by Marry Linke

༄

RANIA—

My name is Rania Bassima Najjar. I am a fifty-two-year-old woman. Born in Beirut. Raised in London. Exiled to Los Angeles.

This story is not about me, although I am a character within. I serve as the greeter, the one who opens the door. I step back from time to time, but then I return. My voice will not be denied. I carry a body/mind/spirit understanding that is superior to most, and it is my duty to share.

But let's begin in the here and now. For I have little hope for the future of mankind. We are on the brink. There are flaws in the human condition, insurmountable flaws. This I know deep in my heart. This is not about religion. Religion fails too many women. No, this is a broader discussion. The discussion of a doomed species, spinning out of control on a tiny planet in an unending universe.

What to make then of this life on Earth?

Many have attempted to address this issue. I have studied their thoughts and found most unsatisfactory. But there is a glimmer here and there—the most comforting to me is this simple maxim—"I am not a body with a soul, but a soul passing through a body."

Well, that's a relief.

But still, it begs the question—What do we do with ourselves? How do we fulfill our mortal needs and desires before our souls pass on to the continuum of life after death? I can only speak for myself. This then is my creed:

First, do no harm. Second, do not underestimate the value of a full stomach and a safe bed. Third, find satisfaction in family, camaraderie, work and the wonders of nature. Fourth, consider that the deepest and highest plane of existence in this mortal life might be found in sexuality.

Ah. I've caught your attention.

So consider this: life is amazing. All life, but especially human life. As if we were made so there was at least someone to appreciate the wonder of it all. And there is only one act that can create a new human life—that is the moment when sperm touches egg. That energy, that force that makes us want to couple, is rich with meaning, primal and spiritual. It is also art.

I am a purveyor of artists, you see. And by adjunct, of sexual beings.

Picasso understood that sexuality is the highest form of art only late in life. Few know what a consummate technical artist he was in his early years. Then his brush grew looser as he entered the Blue and Rose Periods, then it tested the harder line when he burst into Cubism. Then came Guernica and the rest of his masterpieces as he freed his hand and his mind and his heart. Then, having reached the pinnacle of success, how did he spend his final years?

Drawing cunts.

(I abhor vulgarity, but there it is.)

The spreading of thick thighs, the rendering of round bellies. Breasts overflowing with milk and sex. Necks flushed with blood, heads thrown back, mouths agape, lips swollen and damp hair askew. Eyes rolled upwards half shut, or staring. But vaginas, front and center. Not to be denied by bushes of hair or timid curators.

Ah, Picasso. At eighty. At eighty-five. It was as if he had found God.

❧

I live on the eighth floor of the residential tower at the end of San Vicente Boulevard in Santa Monica, California. Safe on the cliff of existence, overlooking the ocean of all oceans.

My husband has been dead for nine years. He was older than me. Imperious. A prickly sort with noble intentions but a short attention span. He was lucky he died suddenly for I had no resolve to nurse him through endless strokes and heart attacks, diapers and pablum. I would have left him. He knew that deep down, and I am grateful that he died accordingly.

So here I live alone. Far from the madding crowd. I see them below in the morning fog, on the manicured paths of the manicured park called Pacific Palisades. The young hardbodies, sprinting past the middle-aged joggers. The dog walkers, holding plastic bags of feces as if they were pastries, stopping to chat as their canines sniff anuses. The old couples shuffling along (many Europeans among them) reasonably secure that out in public among so many fit Americans, there is little chance of a mugging. I have nothing against these people. They are my neighbors.

It's 11 a.m. I've been up for five hours—reading, answering emails and phone calls. But all at a leisurely rhythm, over coffee and a fruit plate. I glide through my morning, glancing out now and again towards the Pacific. Still, the marine layer has not budged. Fog, dense and moist. If the building were only a few stories higher, I would be basking in the sunshine and the view—sweeping South then West—Palos Verdes, Catalina, the Pacific horizon. Then turning to look East across the vast sprawl, Santa Monica, Century City, Beverly Hills, Hollywood, Downtown, then back to the Hollywood sign, clinging to the scrub mountain above Beachwood Canyon.

But fog it is. June Gloom. And this morning I see nothing but grey. I need some color in my life.

I step out of the shower and dry myself. I look in the mirror as always. For fifty-two, my body is holding up well. I'm pleased with it. I keep my ass tight and arms toned at the Santa Monica YMCA. I have no personal trainers in my life. I prefer communal punishment and have no qualms about sharing sweat with strangers.

For an occasion like today's—an informal lunch with a promising young artist—I dress as I always dress—as the exotic modern Lebanese woman I am—fluent in French, English, Hebrew and Arabic, schooled in London, exposed to centuries of culture, and now owner of an art gallery on La Cienega Boulevard. I am very much my own person.

After I dry I lightly lotion. Then I glance through my drawers of underthings. I have a rule. Even on the worst day. When my hair will not come together. When I feel bloat all over. When my face belongs to someone else and again I resist ripping this stupid round hormonal patch off my lower abdomen. I will always, without exception, put on the best underwear in the world.

Always.

I shop hard and find it in the most unlikely places. Rodeo Drive and Target. Lace panties from Thailand. A simple bra that fits my breasts. Cotton, silk, nylon. I have a wide range of lingerie that suits all purposes—a night out with a new man, a quick backpack down Sespe River with Baca, an impromptu lunch with an artist at Bergamot Station who needs my help more than she realizes. My undies will always be there at their best.

But I meander. I mentioned my gallery. It's in the middle of gallery row on La Cienega Boulevard. It's quite prestigious and quite staid. I cater to Middle-Easterners with deep pockets yet surprisingly curious minds. I sell paintings and scrolls from antiquity. I educate these men (and sometimes their wives) in the beautiful art of the Arab and Persian worlds. I take them back into their history—long and glorious—filled with heroic deeds and earthly pleasures.

Then I take their money.

This art pays my rent, but it is not my cup of tea.

When it comes to artists, I like them raw.

ೞ

My old Mercedes sedan cruises up San Vicente Boulevard, the grey growing thinner as the sun burns through. The car fits my purposes. It's reliable and comfortable, and I've found the most reverential Scottish mechanic to service it breathlessly. (Only in Los Angeles.) It smells of history—perfume, tobacco, sex and booze. There are several suspicious stains in the leather seats, front and back. There's room for all, six, seven…including luggage. But no baggage. Not in this car. Here we are free of baggage. We are living, after all, in California.

26th Street—I am heading east. The traffic thickens, but I planned for that. I'm at peace. Why not? I've solved so many of my own problems. Truly. As Americans say, I've got a handle on my life. So I can explore the lives of others and try to be of help.

The sun is strong now. I can feel it in my lap as the old Mercedes moves and slows and moves again. Much of what

I've learned is about the importance of moments like this. How to revel in them. And I do. I let my mind drift to a man in Ojai, pronounced Oh-Hi, whose skin is darker than mine. A Peruvian. His name is Baca. Ah, Baca. I spread my legs a bit, my beautiful silly silk skirt yielding against my thighs. Baca who has taught me so much, but who insists he is an idiot. He likes to laugh. And paint. And take women places. We've been friends for years. When I'm stressed, when I am uncertain, I think of Baca, and I let things go and find my balance again. So here I have Baca in the car with me as I enjoy the sun on my lap and a tingle of anticipation.

She is truly raw, this artist I am about to meet. Maybe too much so. And far too young—twenty-two, twenty-three? Repressed, hyper-active. Filled with pent-up rage and burning ambition. But her saving grace?—she's good. A true painter. And I am intrigued by her.

Her name is Dale and everyone wants a piece of her. She was a student at CalArts when I first learned of her. We met, I looked at her work and we talked. I saw something there, so I set her up—just barely—a space to paint, a few hundred dollars a month for food and necessities. God knows where she's lived over the last couple of years. Let's say she's moved around a lot. But always, she painted. And I encouraged her.

⁂

I was wise to choose Bergamot Station as our meeting place. A cluster of galleries at an abandoned train station in East Santa Monica. Tucked away between the 10 Freeway and Olympic Boulevard. Wise because Bergamot is East of 26th Street, the most reliable dividing line of where you'll find sun if you live in the fog. There's a café there. A cafe worked by smart tattooed young servers, girls and boys, branding themselves with their body art and cool attitudes as the Latinos behind them do the cooking. Am I being unkind? I must write a note to myself—do not be unkind to young people, nor blindly sympathetic to anyone with skin darker than mine.

When I think of Dale, I grow nervous. This is a good sign. A person who puts me on edge is someone worth knowing. So much younger than me. She is tall and awkward and beautiful. Her breasts are small, her ass round. Her long legs restless. Her hair a constant mess.

People like Dale are a challenge to the rest of us: "Here I am! I burn hot. Come mix it up with me." Dangerous, provocative, yet holders of great insight. I personally avoided becoming lovers with her. People like Dale make better friends. But then what am I missing? I am stopped at the light—the left turn arrow onto Michigan Avenue. I daydream. A car horn behind me. I awake and lurch the car forward, left, suddenly dodging among the imposing trucks of the recycling plant, then swinging through the open chain link gates into Bergamot Station. I find myself a parking spot near the café.

I know she'll be late. She is always late. So I'll drop my scarf at the best of the funky tables outside, then walk in and order a mint lemonade from one of the beautiful young servers. Then I'll sit and sip as the sunlight grows warmer and the café begins to fill up for lunch. I'll hear her car before I see her. There will be a cloud of carbon monoxide wafting over the patio as she finally strides up. Adjusting something, tugging on something else. Her clothes, her hair. I can never anticipate her mood. She may be beaming, crying, wary, or filled with deep questions.

As we became friends, we would greet with kisses on each cheek—the cosmopolitan way. She liked that. Then one night we met for dinner at the Border Grill and she strolled in late and came right up to me as I rose from my bar stool and she kissed me on the lips. She offered a fleeting taste of her tongue. And ever since then, that is how we greet each other. No matter where we are. No matter the mood. It is our beautiful public flirtation.

I look forward to it. I step from the Mercedes and cross the parking lot in my sensible open-toe wedge sandals. I stand straight for I am not tall. I scan the outside seating and find a surprise. There she is.

∽

DALE—

Oh, fuck here she is. She's always so fucking put together—I gotta remind myself, it's not about me. Don't go there. It's her, it's Rania. Who she is. That's the beauty of her. She's not dressing for me. She dresses for herself. So maybe I won't kiss her this time. What? Don't go there, don't think like that. That's a game. She's a friend.

I stand as she walks up. I open my arms, we embrace and kiss on the lips, then separate and smile. Then she says, "Dale."

She reaches and touches my cheek and my eyes fill with tears.

"I'm a mess."

"We're all a mess," she answers.

"Yeah, well, what kind of shoes are *you* wearing?"

She laughs. "Dale…"

"No, I'm serious. Tell me."

"They're Manolo Blahnik. I've had them for eleven years."

"And what size are they? They're a four, right? Size fucking four."

Rania stares at me. I'm laughing and smiling, but I'm an asshole and I'm doing it again. I can just be so belligerent and stupid just because. I'm like a fucking teenager. Maybe because she sees through me.

"They are size five. I have corns on my little toes and I need the room."

She smiles and I'm suddenly saying to myself don't cry. Don't cry. I'm not gonna cry. I start crying. And that's what it's like between me and Rania. Just being in her presence, I'm instantly calmer, I mean really I'm laying all this crazy shit on her, but really, for reals, she's making me feel safe. I feel safe here.

"You're hungry," says Rania. She takes my hand and leads me inside where we wait in line then order fancy soup and sandwiches and mint lemonades. There's a guy behind the counter that I fucked a few months ago, but he pretends not to know me. Rania pays, and now we're outside, eating. Rania likes to be conspiratorial. She likes stories. I lean towards her and whisper.

"You know that guy inside? Guy who took our order?"

"I noticed. He's handsome."

"Yeah, well, I fucked him once. Right here on this lot."

"Tell me."

"Friday night opening. Bill's gallery. I forget the artist. So I have a couple vodka cranberries and mix it up a bit, and Bill comes over and you know how he makes things fun, so suddenly we're all having fun, and I'm feeling pretty good, and that guy walks in."

"The guy inside."

"Mr. Food Server Man. So I'd never seen him before, but he's looking like James Dean or somebody. Kinda slouchy and intense, but really killer handsome. And he walks up to me and says, "I want to buy you a drink." And I say, wittingly…I mean like witty, I say, 'That's not all you want.' And he says, 'That's right.'"

Rania is staring at me, hanging on my words, but I'm suddenly lost. The memory has triggered something else, my brain racing away from the moment, and I'm somewhere else—back in some deep, shitty past—and I can't finish the story. But she wants to play it out, "Can I finish it for you?"

"It ends up against a chain link fence," I say.

"I thought as much. He pushed you up against it and raised your skirt and unrolled your underpants. You kissed. Then you undid his belt and unzipped his jeans and you freed him and he entered you and you fucked."

"Yes."

"But you did not come."

"No."

"It was exciting though. Yes? Dangerous."

"Very," I say.

"And you seek that out because…?"

I feel the tears welling again. "Jesus, Rania. Why do you do this to me?! It's like every time we get together it's like a fucking dam-burst! What is it about you!?"

She knows I'm serious. But I'm not accusing her. She knows that too. She thinks about it then says, "I am not sure. We came into each other's lives. We have commonality. You inspire me. Isn't that enough?"

Who the fuck talks like this? This woman is so smart and gracious. And now I'm really crying. She leans forward and whispers, "Tell me."

I do my sob and gasp thing.

"I had some damage happen. Sexual shit. You know. When I was younger."

"I know."

"How do you know?"

"We all have."

"All of us?"

"All of us."

"I'm not painting these days. I can't."

"So then don't. I forbid you."

"Do you?" I stare at her. Sometimes I like being pushed around.

"Yes. Dale, you have deeper work to do. About your past, your trauma."

"Do I?"

"Yes," she says. "Come to Ojai with me. Put down your brushes and come to Ojai and meet my friend Baca. He's a painter, and he's actually quite wise."

"Is he? And he's older, right?"

"My age. Or so he claims."

"Okay, but this guy knows that he's old, right?" (Oh, fuck, here I go again on another stupid rant.) "He's not like one of these guys who's all hey I'm forty-two and I work out, or hey I only just turned fifty, because like they just don't get it—'cause I'm in my twenties right? So anyone older than thirty-five—you're fucking old okay? I don't care how old you are. You're old, so get over it and leave me alone!"

Rania is staring at me. Her mouth is tight and I know I've offended her.

"Oh, God." I feel my eyes welling again, but then that resistance comes out of nowhere—that fuck you thing—why do I even give a shit? But I know why. Because this is Rania Bassima Najjar and she is my friend. "Rania…"

Rania softens her lips, her eyes. "I've known men like that," she says, "from both sides. Men who cannot act their age."

"So, if you take me to Ojai? This guy, Baca, he knows…?"

"He knows what he knows, and he's taught me a lot."

"Does he look like Yoda?"

"No."

"George Clooney?"

"No."

"Younger?"

"Than George Clooney, the same age maybe. He's Peruvian."

"You're driving…?"

"Let's go spend a few days," Rania replies.

BACA—

I try not to let women make me crazy. Because they can do that. It is the way of things between the sexes. Even when they are perfect they will make you crazy. Why? Because of the craziness men have inside. And the weird thing about it, the more perfect a woman, the crazier the man will get.

We seduced people, Rania and me. Opened them up to the higher possibilities of sex and love. Mostly younger. Not always. But we were very good. We danced together with them.

Rania and I met years ago. Instantly there is a connection. We both know that. And so we are lovers for a while and the sex between us, we bring it to a high place. Way up. A high level. Then for Rania suddenly it is we must share the knowledge. It becomes more, "Baca, we must do this. Look at these young people. So ignorant." For me it was stupid, no? Me? A painter. And Rania—she owns a gallery and reads *The Paris Review*. So what are we doing? Sexual healing. Suddenly we are the experts? Rania says yes, of course. She is always sure. So it just happens with the first one. A girl going to a boarding school here in Ojai. The daughter of a friend of Rania's from Israel. She is emotionally alone. The teachers are worried. So Rania picks her up at the school on a Friday and they come here to my place. I make a nice dinner. I compliment this girl. I tell her I want to paint her so of course she grows red and confused. So Rania says, "Baca, make a drawing."

I go for my paper and charcoal, and I sit and I draw this girl. And you know what? With me looking and drawing. And Rania too, this girl, she becomes herself. I see it happen. For Rania it happens too. She sees the girl come awake. It was not a miracle, but close. Later, Rania gives me a wink and I say goodnight. I walk up the hall to my bedroom and I sit on the low large bed. I snap off the light and look out to see Rania and this girl walking through the moonlight of my yard, across the pea gravel and wooden bridge to the hot tub. I hear Rania speaking Hebrew in a whispering way. This girl is all soft now. I watch them take their clothes off then step into the steam and water. I hear Rania whispering again. She is quiet but forceful. She tells me later that she talks to the girl of masturbation. And maybe Rania does a little demonstration, but maybe not, I cannot see because they are low in the hot water. And now Rania will not say. But the girl, after this one night, for her, things are better. When Rania talks of her she gives me all the credit. Just for seeing and drawing her.

And since that time we are "Rania and Baca"—and we have a routine, yes? A sense of what is needed. For people who need some help. And sometimes I say, Rania, enough. Not this weekend. But then she makes me listen to who it is, and so I have the energy for another visit. It's strange, no? It is the way Rania and I make love. Through others.

And now she brings a young woman named Dale.

ひ

RANIA—

Dale is in one of her funks. I know it. I'm picking her up in North Hollywood, in the Valley off the 170. She's been apartment-sitting for a friend, a struggling promoter who's usually out touring with one band or another—a hard-scrabble existence. He insists that she keeps the place neat, and she does. A tidy relationship with no added benefits. I double-park the old Mercedes behind the run-down stucco building and begin to step out. A young tattooed Latino walks from a stairwell with a plastic bag of garbage, heading for the dumpster behind me. I am instantly alert and I stare at him hard. He smiles— "Lady, that is one sweet ride."

I decide he's okay, "Thank you. We decided to grow old together."

He smiles. I dislike being defensive around men, but there are facts that women must face. Neighborhoods like this are filled with men released from prison, out on parole. There are thousands of them. You can look them up on a website and see the clusters of red dots. They have all been traumatized, and some of them are dangerous because of it. But this one, he's okay.

"You here for Dale?" he asks.

"Yes. Do you know her?"

"We used to get high together, but then my wife wasn't cool with it no more. That's one weird chick."

"She's an artist."

He shrugs, "Whatever."

And suddenly she appears—wearing a sleeveless white T-shirt with no bra underneath. Cargo pants and Birkenstocks. She's in one of her pissy moods and I silently groan. She spots my new friend at the dumpster and calls out—"Hey, Manny, don't let any of your douche-bag friends rob the apartment while I'm gone, okay? Please?"

He laughs and yells back, "Yes, ma'am."

She's got an old gym bag stuffed with clothes that she slings into the back seat as she climbs in alongside me.

"Good morning," I say.

"We've been robbed twice in the last six months."

This makes my point. This is no way for a woman to live. Life's journey is outward, but also inward. There is no possibility of you exploring your inner being if you are always protecting yourself, always on the defensive. To realize what lies within, you must be in a safe place.

Do I say this to Dale? No. Because I know her response: "What am I supposed to fucking do then?!" And she has a point. These young artists, they live without any money. It is

14

hard. I can only smile sympathetically, pull my beautiful car out and down the street and we're off to Ojai. West on the 101 through the Valley, Van Nuys, Encino, Thousand Oaks, down Conejo Grade, Camarillo, Oxnard. The fog of Ventura offering just a glimpse of the ocean, then up the 33 and back into the sunshine as we enter the Ojai Valley. I won't attempt a description of this place. It would seem full of platitudes. You'll grow to know Ojai page by page. A tidbit here, a morsel there. It's better that way. Ojai is a valley after all, a woman, and she prefers that you get to know her gradually.

ᘓ

DALE—

Fuck this. Fuck Manny. Fuck my friend's apartment with all the locks and window bars. Fuck Rania and fuck her precious fucking Mercedes, fuck Ojai and fuck Baca.

ᘓ

BACA—

Saturday mornings I head downtown for coffee and some talk at Ojai Roasting. There are several groups of friends who meet here. I move easily among them. It's so easy for me, and it is my pleasure to be gracious with people. I think they are open to me because I look different, but also because I pay attention to detail.

I come for coffee here also because sometimes my son comes here. We are close and yet far. And sometimes the best way to meet is like this. Not planned. He comes here because Stacey hires only quality girls as baristas. She says to them, look at you, you are smart and sexy so you are hired. And then, because they are safe behind the counters, yes? They push up their breasts and show skin, and piercings, and they are young and sly and wise, no? So my son comes in sometimes. And men like me. To flirt and feel good. And women, who know Stacey, and also feel comfortable here.

So here I am, among friends, waiting for who shows up first.

✌

DALE—

I ride it out. And slowly all the stress and shit slips away. I lean back, close my eyes, kick off my Birks and put my feet up on the leather dashboard in the sun. Rania drives, talking on about past love affairs. It's like this droning oral history, talking about partners she was with, and it's all about how they smelled and what they were wearing and how things went. And it's kinda dreamy, so I go into this trance thinking, okay, so my life is a fucking train wreck, okay? So I'm driving up to Ojai to get out of my own way, right? Whatever that means. Trying to break out of some rut. And I'm with the one person I trust more than anyone in the world, so I just gotta go with this one. It feels all right. So I reach over and take her hand. And we hold hands as she drives. Like a couple of African men on a walk somewhere.

RANIA—

When a girl holds my hand like this, I cannot tell you the pleasure. It isn't sexual, but it is. It feels good in a nice girly way. At times like this when I can glance over and study her features, I see how Dale truly is. Her brown hair neither short nor long, but going every which way, then her exquisite forehead, strong brows over hooded eyes, a Roman nose and beautiful full lips. I see her and I imagine her. I imagine her small breasts under her white T-shirt. I've seen her nipples swell. And I look down over her round belly and wide hips. As long as I've know her, I've

16

never seen her naked. But I've imagined being with her. Those long legs of hers. Intertwining our bodies. I've imagined that and that's not my fault, it's Dale's. Because she gets everyone imagining that.

So now we're up the 33 and past the Y and heading into downtown Ojai. It's of a piece, this place. Sunny, funky, charming, but with a fierce guard up against the sprawl of Los Angeles, only ninety minutes away. Baca asked for us to meet him at Ojai Roasting. He wants to show us off. I think of Baca. My Baca. "He wants to show us off, you know," I say to Dale, still holding her hand.

"Yeah?"

"It's quite innocent. He'll tell you—to be sitting there among his friends when we walk in, that will be satisfying to him. Confirmation."

"Of what?"

"His understanding of yin."

"So he is Yoda."

We laugh.

☙

BACA—

I'm in the coffee house with my friends, and they come in and I stand up and of course always it is a pleasure to see Rania. Always. We kiss and hug and then Rania presents Dale. And this girl, she is to the moon, you know. I mean, this is the girl, everyone wants her. It's like give me a piece of this. So when we are introduced, I open my arms to her, why not? She gives me a smile, but then turns to my friends and says, "Is this guy safe!? Yes or no!?" It is funny and charming and my friends laugh and half of them shout "Yes!" and half shout "No!" And she says, "I'll take that for a yes!" And she gives me a great hug. And that's what this girl will do to you. Knock you off your balance.

But with my body pressed up against her, I can feel the resistance within her. It's as clear to me as cold water. We laugh and separate, but I see the flush in Dale's neck. She knows why she is here. But me? Why am I involved now with this one? This one is a piece of work. So maybe for this one I will let Rania carry the weight. We'll see.

DALE—

This guy Baca is all right by me. He's got a good vibe. I knew he would. 'Cause of Rania. She hates flakey people. Uh, no, it's more like she doesn't introduce flakey people to each other. Anyway, it felt fine hugging him and meeting his friends. Then we step out onto the sidewalk and the sun is freakin' hot. We're supposed to follow Baca up to his house when a van rolls by with surfboards on top, and this young guy leans halfway out the window and he's all tan with crazy hair and bright blue eyes and he yells, "Rania! You don't write, you don't call! I love you! I love you!"

Rania stares and frowns, but then she like gathers herself and shouts back, "I love you too, Emilio!"

"Who was that?" I ask.

Rania shoots Baca a weird look. "My son," says Baca. "Emilio."

"So, he's part of the deal too?"

They both laugh.

"He should be so lucky," says Rania.

Rania and I climb back into the Mercedes and we follow Baca in his Volvo back out of town and up this straight road, up and up, under oak trees, past rock-walled homes and bursting gardens. Until we finally make a left onto a long driveway, and when I look over I see a long, low house through the trees—whitewashed plaster and a red tile roof. Broad wood windows that capture the sun through the trees. I see it all—the flagstone, the lounge chairs, the pool and Jacuzzi and

18

flowering plants everywhere. And I'm thinking to myself, what the fuck am I doing here, and I answer—something else. I'm doing something else.

Baca is sweet to us. He shows us our rooms then gives us ten minutes to unpack and wash up before meeting back in the kitchen. I follow his orders. He's cutting up a baguette and some cheese and salami. He slices a tomato and separates some fresh basil. He offers me a glass of wine. Rania's still in her room. I'm starving and so is Baca and we both eat fast, laughing. Swilling Chardonnay.

"So what are we doing here?" I ask.

"Only what you are ready for."

"And that's some kinda rule?"

"Of course. Rules are good. They make us safe. The understanding."

"You know, Rania says that you can help me get past some blocked up shit I'm carrying."

"I hope she isn't making any promises."

"No. She just thought I should come."

"So you're here. Okay. So, I think you can do this.

"Do…?"

"Look, it's simple. You come here and first you relax. Just relax."

"And that's all I have to do?"

"What? No, that's just the first day. Then tomorrow we will show you a few things about yourself. Things we have learned. Things that help. But I don't go into the past. See for me, it is not all in the brain that you carry these things. I don't know how to talk about the brain and how to help that. But I know that also it is in your body, this. You carry it in places, and here maybe we can help."

"Oh."

I gotta admit, my mouth is open. I'm staring at him. Has anyone even bothered describing him? He has dark eyes, brown

19

skin, black hair. He's clean-shaven. Medium height, lean build. Strong forearms. Wearing a white polo shirt, jeans and huaraches. He's easy to be with. I'm going into a trance again. Staring at this man as I stand in his kitchen.

"So listen. I have some work to do in my studio. But *mi casa es su casa*, no? So relax. And go give Rania a shake. You two go sit naked by the pool. She likes that. With a girl like you, to lay naked in the sun and talk about things."

So that's what I do. I knock and Rania comes to the door in a bathrobe. I follow her to the kitchen where she stops and observes the mess Baca and I have left. She tears off a piece of baguette, smears it with cheese and eats it. "I'm starving," she says.

I laugh. "I thought you were so elegant."

"Girl, I'm in Ojai now." So I watch as she eats, then we carry the wine out towards the pool. When we step from the shade the sun is very warm.

"It's okay to get naked?" I ask.

Rania says yes. So I strip off my top and pants and panties and leap into the pool and it's fucking colder than I expected and I'm suddenly shrieking. Then I turn to Rania. She's standing at the edge in her white robe. "Come in, chickenshit." Rania steps from her robe and leaps in. We're both fucking screaming because it really is cold. Then we're scrambling out onto the hot flagstone and we're lying there between the sun and the stone, shivering and warming up and smiling.

"You have a beautiful body," I tell her.

"Thank you. So do you."

"No, I don't. I have parts."

"Beautiful parts then."

"Yeah."

RANIA—

And she's right. Her parts are still not in sync. But she's lovely and beautiful and bold to be here. I feel my heart going out to her even more. We move to the lounge chairs with their warm soft cushions and lie back, open to the sun and we close our eyes. "We can't fall asleep here." I say.

"I know."

"Only long enough to dry, then we must move out of the sun."

"Okay."

I glance over at Dale. She's staring at the sky, hands over her head. Stretched out like that, her breasts nearly disappear except for the nipples, her usually round belly grows flat, her hip bones stick out and between them an untrimmed bush of dark pubic hair. Her thighs are soft, tapering into lean calves and long white feet.

She's beautiful, this girl. I speak to her. "Dale, hey, Dale?"

"What?"

"It's nice to be naked with you."

"Yeah, okay."

"I have no sexual intentions."

"Aw, man."

"This is a good place for you and me. To be naked but not touching. We can talk, okay? So now, some of what we have learned, Baca and me, is about anatomy. That is the simple trick of it. First to know your body."

"Okay."

"Okay, then do this. Don't resist. Just do as I say. Pull your knees up halfway."

"Okay."

"Now touch the soles of your feet together and let your knees spread apart." She follows my directions. "You've opened yourself, yes? To the sun."

"Yes."

"So just listen to me now. You feel the sun on you. You've spread your legs. So now close your eyes and just feel that. Okay. Feel the sun on you."

And that is what we do. Such an open-soul pleasure. To be safe and open to the warm rays of the sun. And after a delicious ten, fifteen minutes I say, "Now it is time to cover up and go inside."

"Aw…"

"We mustn't burn ourselves."

"So that's it?"

"That's it. End of lesson two."

"What was lesson one?"

"Making sure that Manny didn't steal my car."

℃

BACA—

We are going out for dinner. I don't know how, but somehow Rania finds something beautiful for Dale to wear. From the hall closet she keeps for herself in my house. Rania has this way with clothes. Layering and wrapping. But later she told me something strange. This girl Dale's hair, it is always going every which way, no? But when Rania offered to fix it, apply a bit of gel maybe, she suddenly grew very *agitada*. And Rania, of course, backed off. I don't know why this catches my attention.

So we are finally off to Azu. An excellent tapas restaurant with a good bar but sometimes shaky service. I know because my boy Emilio works there some nights. But not tonight.

We take my Volvo because her big Mercedes is a pain to park. Besides, Rania is my guest and it is nice for her not to drive. I keep the Volvo clean. Dale sits in the back, Rania alongside me. I glide the car down Foothill and work my way through the side streets to Ojai Avenue. A break in the traffic,

I go left, and in six minutes we are parking. No valet. We walk into the restaurant and turn a few heads—Oly, from the Monday night poker game. Kim and a friend, actors, sharing drinks and making plans. Barclay's daughter, Hope, tending bar. I say hello but do not introduce my lady friends.

We are escorted to the back room where we sit and scan menus. We are relaxed with a slight edge, but I will say we all feel good. So we drink some red wine from Chile and share some tapas. Eating and jabbering about nothing. It is fun but there is much question in the air between us. I don't know what to think. What to do about this girl. She's messy and tricky. She is very seductive. I see how Rania falls for her and it pains me a bit. Maybe in a good way. I don't know. Like I say, I don't know what to think. Over dinner we slide into the talk about trust. Rania and I have this down. We are funny and play off each other—doing a little strip tease, no? Of our own lives. In front of Dale. Until she is laughing and her body relaxes. But like I say, she is tricky. As the night grows late, Rania takes Dale's hand and says, "Dale, you know you are here for a reason." She nods yes. We enter into silence.

Can we help her? Maybe. Will we pay a price? Probably. Will there be a reward? Yes. There is always a reward for trying.

⁂

DALE—

So I've eaten too much and drank too much red wine. Hello. Welcome to my world. But I'm not in North Hollywood anymore. I'm in Ojai, with Rania and Baca and they're driving me back to his house, and I'm thinking, these two better not have some kinky shit planned here and just then Baca says, "Dale, for you tonight, Rania will help you into bed, okay? With a glass of water and two aspirin."

"Okay," I answer.

And that's what happens. Because I am kinda wobbly, but Rania gets me unwrapped then makes me swallow some aspirin with the water, then hands me a beautiful cotton nightgown and she helps me strip naked and pull it on up over my head. Then she turns and pulls back the bed covers and I climb into a big, high, luxurious bed, with perfect white sheets and white down comforter and embroidered pillow cases. I am content and very relaxed. Rania strokes my face. "You're safe here, Dale. You will fall asleep safe and wake up safe. You are safe to dream. You can spread your legs, but do not touch yourself."

"What?"

"Listen to me," Rania whispers. You may touch your breasts a bit. And you may spread your legs. But do not touch yourself. It's no big deal. But no fingers down there."

"Then I'll dream it."

Rania changes. "You can control your dreams?"

"Sometimes. If I think about something enough going to sleep, I'll dream it."

"Hah," says Rania. "Baca will be interested in this."

"Yeah?"

"Yeah. So dream good thoughts tonight. I'll tell him."

She kisses me on the lips. I open my mouth and offer my tongue but she whispers goodnight and she's gone.

So of course in a minute I'm squirming all over this delicious bed, feeling the wine and the warm company and what it's like to sleep without sirens and helicopters and drunk assholes in the street. It really is fucking peaceful. And warm. I touch my breasts and it feels good. I spread my legs, but I obey Rania and I don't go there. And it makes me feel free in this strange way. I have been ordered not to touch myself. I spend a strange restless night, twisting in the sheets, tangling my legs, dreaming dreams I won't remember.

RANIA—

It is almost midnight. I meet Baca in the kitchen where he is making tea. "So what do you think?" I ask him.

"I don't know. She's like a boy in a way. She's going different directions."

"Yes, but she is no boy. What works with the others will work with her."

"Rania, you have fallen in love with her."

"Of course. And so will you."

"Not me, baby, I'm playing hard to get."

I laugh. This man is full of surprises. But always in balance. I don't know how he does it. All these women I have brought to him, he is always smooth, and when he reaches a limit, he excuses himself and goes off alone. Often as a guest is in mid-sentence. But nobody holds it against him because he is being Baca. As well as I know him, he is still a mystery. Sometimes, when I am impatient, I think he's a charlatan. But maybe that's what people need. Baca the Magnificent, to pull the veil away.

I smile at him and kiss him on the lips. "You know what I want to do tonight?"

"Tell me."

I want to sleep in your bed, with the window open, under the comforter, naked, on our sides, and I want to snuggle up against you and wrap an arm around you and press my breasts into your back and feel my yoni against your ass and go to sleep like that. How does that sound?

"Beautiful," he says.

"But promise if you are going to fart, you will first roll over."

He laughs. "How can I promise this? I am asleep."

"You'll find a way. You are Yoda."

We laugh. We can be stupid like this together. Then we grow quiet. Standing there in the kitchen. We hug and breathe deeply. And in these fleeting quiet moments of togetherness and reflection, pressed up against each other like this, we both return to the many memories from our sexual history. I may go here, he may go there. But it is all ours. And no one can ever take that away from us.

After our tea, Baca and I retire to his bedroom and do exactly as I described, but no sooner than we are naked and I am pushed up against him then he farts. On purpose. He must have held it from the kitchen. And we laugh and I say thank God we opened the window.

But later, as we're drifting off, I remember something, and I whisper, "Baca, Dale told me she can control her dreams."

"Really."

"Yes. That interests you?"

"We are such stuff as dreams are made on; and our little life is rounded with sleep."

"So you and Shakespeare."

"That's right, baby. Me and Wild Bill."

"Goodnight, Baca. Love of my life."

"Goodnight."

&

DALE—

It's morning. The birds are fucking chirping. I wake up and I'm feeling like I could go either way. I've got this cranky thing going, okay? But then, I realize I'm feeling pretty good actually, so I start telling myself okay I'm just scared. So big deal I'm scared to be here with Rania and this Baca guy. 'Cause they have plans for me. Then I say fuck it, and I get out of bed and head to the bathroom and pull up my nightie and sit and pee then brush my teeth and walk down the hall to the kitchen.

26

No one's there. I look down into the living room. Nobody. Then I look out into the backyard and they're sitting there in bathrobes with their feet up at a round table with coffee and newspapers. Arguing about economics or something.

I step out. "Good morning."

They turn and Rania smiles and says, "Good morning, Dale."

It feels nice to hear her say my name. But Baca, he's looking at me like who are you? Then he says, "Good morning. In the kitchen you will find some food."

Rania jumps in, "Baca, I will help her."

"She can help herself." Baca turns to me, "Yes?"

"I can help myself," I say. Then he stares at me.

"And you know why you are here." It's forceful and direct. "Yes."

"So in one hour, in the studio, we will go to work, the three of us. And you will not resist, yes?" I stare at him. My eyes do not well with tears. I feel safe and hungry to make a change.

"Yes."

Baca stares at me then suddenly smiles. A smile that just melts me in this weirdest fucking way, then he says, "You know. Dale. That's it. The first time you receive me. The first time." He turns to Rania, "The first time!" he says.

Rania smirks a bit and mutters something about Yoda, but I know what Baca's talking about. And I feel a glow in me. I turn and head for the kitchen. Rania calls out, "Dale, there is fruit and granola and yogurt," and I hear Baca barking at Rania to shush and listen to the point he was making. And I'm thinking just go with the flow here girl 'cause what's the worst that could happen? I'm heading off into God knows what. But better here than Hollywood, stepping off one more wrong curb, too high and too late on the wrong fucking night.

RANIA—

The studio is away from the house. Up a slope in a grove of pepper trees. The path is again made of pea gravel, and I find it annoying as we crunch our way up. Whose idea was this? Pea gravel. I think, maybe it is some Zen test for me, "You must master the crunch," but then I come to my senses, knowing that no, it is just a short-sighted idea of some small-minded landscape architect and now we all have to suffer because it looks good and it's cheap. (*Mon Dieu*, listen to me babble on this morning.) But I am excited too, at the prospect of this first session. As we head up single file to the studio, Baca, Dale, then me. Because of Dale. But also, because I saw the spark in Baca at the table, that look in his eye, and now I see the power in his stride and it infuses me as well. The power of persuasion and release.

ை

DALE—

So I don't know why shit like this matters, what people are wearing, but Rania told me that I should just wear a t-shirt and my undies and some loose shorts, right? 'Cause I was thinking, I don't know what I was thinking, like they'd have some ceremonial robe for me or some shit. And Baca, it looks like he's wearing the same thing he wore last night, white polo shirt and jeans and huaraches. And somehow that takes a little of the freak out of it. And Rania, she's dressed sensible too, but always you know, she's always got that style thing happening. She just oozes it and I'm like fuck you, I can never pull that off, but again, it's Rania. It's not me and I'm just grateful to be her friend.

So we step up onto this flat deck with no railings, and there are these soft mats around, and the studio looks kinda

Japanesey—with these big sliding doors all opened up, and so it's inside out. And the morning sun is coming through the pepper trees and I follow Baca up the steps and I'm still feeling okay, bring it on. Lay it on me. Whatever it is.

RANIA—

I'm the last into the studio but then I take charge, not Baca. It is part of our routine. We will shift Dale from the masculine to the feminine and back again. It was not something we ever calculated. We just did it one time, years ago, when first Baca became tired, than me, and so we stepped in for each other. We saw that it worked. The ebb and flow. The Yin and Yang.

I play the yin well because I am the yin. It is my nature. I am a woman first and foremost and for all.

I see that Dale is finally showing some receptiveness. Looking around the studio. Natural light and bamboo floors, flowers and art. A broad floor to ceiling mirror on one wall, and against the opposite wall, Baca's paints and easels and stacks of canvasses, all turned away. And finally, against the third wall, across the clean bamboo floor, a large red futon, its back half-raised. "What do you think?"

"It's beautiful."

"It was designed as a place of expression. Here, help me light incense."

I know how Dale is tactile so I hand her a stick of incense and box of wooden matches.

"Try to light it with one match," I say. And this way I am focusing her intent. This studio is not just a place for dreams. As far as I have learned helping women, if you first give them a task, some ritual focus, this will help put them at ease, and immediately other places in the body that are holding too tight will begin to release.

So Dale lights the incense and stands there, staring as the thin line of white smoke wafts up into the rafters. "Blow out the match before it burns you," I say.

She does.

"There are many more matches to light. An infinite number." I study Dale's face, half-expecting a skeptical smirk. But she is in the moment.

"Okay, let's sit then, and talk this through." The bamboo floor is hard under our feet, so we wait as Baca takes three mats from the deck and carries them inside and arranges them in a triangle. They hold the warmth of the morning sun. We all sit, legs crossed and look from one to another. "Here's how it will go," I say. "We will do some breathing exercises, and some stretching, and I'll talk some about the different practices, Tantra, the reality of chakra and others, and how there are ways to access energy centers in your body, and how to get there. I'll talk about how every ancient culture had sexual rituals, and teachers who were devoted to sharing the knowledge. Then we'll take a break—stand up and stretch and drink some water and do toilet if we have to. We will step out onto the deck and enjoy the sun."

"And then?" Dale asks.

"Then Baca, with your permission, will put his hands on your body."

I stare at Dale, awaiting her reaction. She is staring at Baca as if they are playing poker.

"It is not a massage exactly. He has a way of finding places that need release. It is not sexual. He will touch you everywhere to discover where you are holding things. Then he'll rub them out."

"Okay," says Dale.

"We will all be gentle with each other and we'll talk it through, okay? As we go."

"Okay."

So I lead Dale and Baca through a series of breathing and stretching and reaching exercises. And I whisper to her about opening up her frame, her skeleton, and stretching the parts away from each other so the internal parts have some room, and she does well, her breathing growing slower and steadier, a nice warm glow flushing her neck and cheeks. I talk of the seven different chakras, from head to pelvis, and how each requires attention and how you can move each breath up and down your spine, moving from one chakra to another, drawing and releasing energy.

Twenty, thirty minutes pass. I glance over, worried that Baca may be falling asleep, but no, he gives me a look and I know his knee is hurting so I return my attention to Dale and slowly lead her out of this breath-meditation and back to us. She looks relaxed, open. I say, "So now a little break."

Dale turns to Baca. "And then it's your turn?"

Baca is all seriousness. Staring into Dale's eyes. "Will you take your clothes off in front of us? Rania and me?"

Dale hesitates. Baca continues, "It is a very important step. We both have the eyes of artists. We see everything physical about you. Everything."

"Without judgment," I say.

Baca shoots me a look. "Of course, without judgment. But we know this step is good. Then I will put my hands on you, with coconut oil, and maybe Rania will rub your feet."

"I would love to rub your feet."

"And I'll see if I find anything. It's just knots, you know. But somehow, I know when they should be rubbed away, so we see."

"Okay. And after that?"

"After that we eat."

BACA—

A girl like Dale, she is modest but she is not. About her body. Rania and I watch as she takes her clothes off in front of us. It's a quiet moment. I see tears come to her eyes. Rania understands this better than me. I look to Rania. She says, "Dale, you are safe with us. You are beautiful. You have a beautiful body."

She smiles, "Thanks."

Rania continues. "Now come lie on your stomach on this table and Baca will put his hands on you."

Dale says okay like in a trance. She lies down on a massage table and Rania is whispering, close your eyes, breathe up and down your spine. I take some oil in my palms and with great tenderness, I begin exploring her body. I have the touch for this. The feel. Maybe it is the anatomy classes, maybe the painting. I don't know. But I can see and know her with my fingers and palms. Her long ropy muscles under her skin. With pockets of flesh. Her bones are big through her hips. And so delicate through her hands and feet that I wonder how they don't break. I touch her all over, gently, but digging in.

After a while Dale says, "Finding anything?"

Rania laughs and says, "Baca?"

I say, "Yes."

Dale, she squirms a bit and says, "Rania...?"

"You don't want me to rub your feet. Too many hands."

"Come talk to me. Whisper in my ear that it's okay."

So Rania goes and kneels before Dale and whispers in her ear as I explore this body which is so outstanding, and everywhere I am finding knots. Large like a walnut in some places. More of them like an almond or a black bean. And some as small as a grain of rice. And it is these mostly, the little ones, that I know need help. Because when my fingers find them, Dale, she jumps and tries to cry out, but then she swallows her cry. As Rania whispers in her ear. You can cry out. You can cry out. And so she does.

DALE—

Man, this is fucking weird. But I'm buying into all of it, okay? The whole touchy-feely Ojai thing. And now I've got this fucking handsome Peruvian shaman guy with his hands all over me, and it all feels okay until his fingers find something gnarly and my whole body freaks in pain. But then he circles his fingers around it, adding more oil, and Rania reminds me to breathe, breathe. He works three fingers, then two. And then it is only one finger, circling, working around and around, and I begin to cry. Because it's so tender and he works it and works it and I'm just crying and crying and Rania's whispering, it's okay, sweetie, it's good, it's good to cry...

ↄ

BACA—

And this girl, Dale. Man, this girl's got a lot of rice and beans.

ↄ

RANIA—

Finally Baca is done. Dale is wobbly as she stands and I slip a cotton blanket over her. "Are you okay with the oil on your skin? Do you want to shower?"

"I'm okay," she says. "I just want to be quiet."

Baca declares—"I'm making lunch." And he strides out and off the deck and down the pea gravel path like a plumber onto his next appointment. Dale pulls on her clothes and we walk along, my arm around her, and halfway to the main house we sit in the shade of a pine tree where Baca has built a bench. The sun is much higher and the heat is rising. This is Ojai.

Dale is quiet. I take her hand.

"Are you okay?"

"Yeah."

"So Baca will make us a nice lunch, then you and I will go back to the studio. And we will move through the next step. Just us. This step is all yin. I will teach you all you need to know about yourself. Physically. Your pussy and all its parts."

She scrunches her face, "Right after lunch?"

I laugh and say, "You've got to do this work, honey. Listen, you are lucky that you have us to lend a hand. Most women, when they become aware, they are doing this work on the bathroom floor with a mirror and the children screaming."

"And some asshole yelling for his dinner."

"Yes. Like Manny."

We laugh then Dale mock-frowns and says, "Hey, Manny's my friend."

"Mine too. He didn't kill me or steal my car."

We smile and hold hands, each knowing that really, in the real world, men like Manny are heroes.

Baca finally calls us and by now Dale has her vigor back, so we head down the path to the main deck where Baca has set lunch. It's mostly fruit, peeled and sliced and cool. Sparkling water. But then there's a plate of fresh grunion that he caught down at Rincon after a full moon. He's poached them and chopped them up with some weird peppers and he shows us how to smear it on matzo and of course it is delicious and goes great with the cold red grapes.

"Poor man's caviar," he says, but Dale is just eating and being quiet.

DALE—

I'm a little in shock, I gotta say. My whole body is feeling different. My skin is buzzing and I'm dizzy. And it's hot out and now the food, and how these two people are being so good to me, but really I just want to curl up into a ball. I just want to nap. I'm done for the day, I'm done. So they let me nap. But just for an hour. Rania leads me into a grove to a hammock and shows me a trick about how not to fall out and I climb in and I'm asleep.

RANIA—

Baca and I clear the plates and do the kitchen. Everything is modest and sensible in his kitchen. Organics go into a compost bin. Water is used sparingly. In a moment all is clean and we are leaning against the tile counter and I can see that Baca is tired. But also worried. "What?" I ask.

"You're gonna do your mirror thing now?"

"Yes," I answer. "Why?"

"I don't know. She is emotional."

"So? More reason."

"I don't know, that's all. I need a rest."

"So go rest."

"And after that?" says Baca. "When you're done? How about I take her into town? To Ojai Beverage for a glass of wine."

"You think that is good for her?"

"One glass," Baca says, "Then across the street to Westridge and we'll buy a small chicken to grill, yes? And some greens, and I'll make her choose a Pinot Noir.

"Okay. I think she'll like that."

"So, anything else I can do now? Polish your mirrors or something?"

I smile and kiss him. I kiss him deeply and push my body into his. "I love you, Baca."

"*Je t'aime*," he says, his only words of French.

I turn away and go sit in the garden alongside Dale in her hammock, and I wait for her to waken. I contemplate what comes next and feel a rush. I love this next step. It brings me the greatest satisfaction.

∞

DALE—

So I'm awake, sorta. Rania leads me back into the studio and over to the red futon. I'm dreamy and warm and half asleep still. Then we sit down side by side on the futon, the back tilted up, and we lean back and swing our feet up. She takes my hand and we stare out over the garden and she starts talking.

"Close your eyes and listen. Some of this you will know and some you won't know. You are safe here. And warm. For women, this is the first and foremost condition to finding your sexuality. And before you go further, it is important that you truly learn what is going on down there. Inside and out."

"You mean my pussy?" I ask.

"Yes. Your beautiful pussy. Your yoni. A prettier word for it. It's Sanskrit, from the Hindus who knew much and who used the word only with reverence. And as I talk about it, I want you to slowly undress and spread your legs. Then I'll give you some lube and as I become specific you can finger the places I am talking about. Yes?"

"Yes." I say. "But can you take your clothes off too?"

I'm thinking Rania might freak here but she doesn't. "Of course." She stands up and steps out of her shorts and panties and lays them on the floor. Her bush is trimmed, the hair brown and red. Then she pulls her shirt over her head and drapes it over her shorts. She's like so fucking cool getting

36

naked. She's so fucking perfect. She unsnaps her bra and frees her breasts and smiles at me and shakes them a bit. She sits back down alongside me and stretches her legs out and starts talking. "Every yoni is the same and every yoni is different." I raise my hips and begin pulling my shorts off. Rania goes on, "This special area of your body is yours. It should be appreciated and loved. And always protected. From now on it will only be touched when it is ready and willing to be touched. Agreed?"

"Yes," I say. I pull down my panties and lay them on my shorts, then do the same with my t-shirt. I lie back down and feel the glow of the afternoon and the trance of Rania's words.

"Now, spread your legs again and let's begin."

RANIA—

And so I move through my usual recitation. How women are absolutely connected to the moon and their menstrual cycle. How if we get in touch with that, it will ease the way in daily life. "That and moving to a new apartment," says Dale. I laugh and shush her.

And then I move on to the genitalia. I squeeze some lube into her palm and tell her to dab two fingers and explore herself while I talk. And quietly and in great detail I discuss the labia, the clit, the urethra. And then the vagina and all the erectile tissue that surrounds it. I speak of the various paths to orgasm and of the need to have all the parts working together. I speak of how women take control of their sexuality by exploring their anatomy and how only through understanding comes fulfillment. And only through looking and feeling can we understand.

DALE—

Okay, so I'm into this. I have no reason to freak out. Rania turns and reaches for a hand mirror on a small table. She's naked, right? Her body is beautiful—her breasts, the way her back meets her ass. I've only been with a woman when there's another guy there. A couple times. I never was alone with one. I can imagine Rania. I feel the blood rush. She scoots down the futon, sitting alongside my hips now, spreading my legs with her hands and angling the mirror.

"Sit up," she says, "So you can see yourself."

I look at my hairy puss in the mirror. "Wow, somebody call Supercuts."

Rania laughs. "Maybe I will give you a little trim later. But for now, look. Take a long look at yourself. And this will be a routine that you must do every day. Take a mirror and look. And touch. Look at your body as you come out of the shower. Look over your shoulder at your ass. If you are to expand sexually it is only as you come to know and see and love your beautiful pussy and your beautiful body."

"Okay. All right. I'm down with that."

"So, back to the moving parts."

She tells me all about what's going on down there, and I'm looking and groping around, and after a while I start to understand what this is all about. It's not some intellectual thing, it's just like, lying on a futon here with my legs spread and a teacher going through it, so natural, I'm just getting a nice sense of things. I feel like Rania and Baca might actually know what they're doing. And then she kind of loses me talking about the urethra and erectile tissue and that how some women squirt. I say to her, "I'm kinda not gettin' this squirt thing."

"You are aware, though?"

I say, "I've seen the video."

"For now, it is not a goal, but it is important for you to have the physical knowledge of it. That it is real and natural."

"You mean like six old chicks wearing leather in some kind of circle jerk, squirting all over each other."

"What videos have you been watching?"

"Manny's."

We laugh.

But then I'm like, just promise to get me off, all right? Just help me because I get so close, again and again, and my head fills with blood and I'm fucking grinding my teeth but I can't release. I can't release. I can't release.

❧

BACA—

Man, I'm waking up with a hard-on to make any man proud. Because I know what's going on in the studio. I've been dreaming about it during this nap. And when I hear that Dale, she can somehow control her dreams, I'm thinking, that's where I'm going. Maybe that can solve a lot of problems. Like, if you are married, you can still have sex with someone else, but only in your dreams. Make it a purposeful act. With intention, as Rania always says. Anyway, this hard-on, I will let it quiet down. As a man gets older, it's not so important to ejaculate as to keep the arousal level. When I stay aware and in the world, but I do not come, I begin to see sex in everything and that's okay by me.

❧

RANIA—

I can see Dale is in pain. On a quest for orgasm—but like most women, she is getting ahead of herself. She must return to what is. Baca says to me sometimes that maybe it is not so important doing this mirror work with women, but I am convinced that it is. He says sex can be like driving a nice car, you don't need to understand the engine to enjoy the ride. But then he talks like a man. For women, it is different. We must not only be drivers, but we must be mechanics of our own engines. To truly understand how complex it all is down there between your legs, to see the anatomy of our beautiful sexual engines, is the first step to truly experience our sexuality.

I am pleased so far with Dale. Her spirit of openness. Her playfulness. She loses focus sometimes, but that is her brain interrupting. She will learn to control that with breathing.

"Okay, so now regain your focus, yes? Regain your focus."

"Regaining focus."

"Your vagina is central to your entire identity as a woman. It receives a man and delivers a child. It is a multi-tasker and it is a sacred place. Again, you must honor it and protect it." Dale is inserting her fingers into her vagina. I tell her to wait and I take her middle finger and squeeze on some more lube.

"So, only one finger."

"You do it," she pleads. "You touch me. You show me."

"No. This is your work. I am only the guide here."

So I have her explore herself as I discuss the erectile tissue to be found—first down along the vaginal floor. Then from side to side where she finds the vestibular bulbs along the vaginal walls. Capable of swelling, growing aroused. I see her cheeks growing flushed, her closed eyes fluttering as her single finger explores. "Now," I say, "Turn your wrist so your knuckles turn down and reach your fingertip up, just beyond the entrance to your pussy."

"The G spot," she says.

"You know it?"

"Not a clue."

"It's there," I say. "It is not a myth."

"What does it feel like?"

"It depends. It varies from woman to woman. During arousal, it will engorge with blood and feel spongy to the touch. About the size of a nickel, a quarter... It is no magic button, but another place to grow to know and love."

"I can't find it," she says. "Help me."

She turns her head, her eyes pleading almost. I smile. "Okay, then together we'll find it. I spread her labia with two fingers. She is wet with lube and her own secretions, her middle finger still in her pussy. I slip mine in underneath it and she gasps. "Easy," I say. "Are you okay?"

"Yes."

"Okay, now let's do this, our two fingers exploring together. First we push deep inside, yes, then up, and then we crook our fingers as if saying come here to someone, and with pressure we slowly pull the finger back towards the entrance, and somewhere along here we…"

"Ahhh. Oh, ahhhh."

"Yes. There. There it is." Dale lies there, quivering, until I feel her finger back away from the spot and join mine below. She exhales deeply.

"Will there be a quiz?" Dale asks.

I laugh and say no, but that I have left a book on her nightstand that I expect her to look through. She seems content with that. I pull my finger from her pussy and wave it in the air.

Dale lies there naked, legs spread, skin flushed with sex and sun, a finger still inside her. She looks at me, a little spacey-eyed and says, "Are you gonna kiss me later?"

I take her wrist and pull her finger from her vagina and lay her hand across her belly. There is a rich smell of musk in the air.

"For women, sexuality is a warm ocean. The water washes over you and in you and through you. There is no hiding from it once you immerse yourself. It will find every crack and crevice, it will ooze into you until you cannot resist anymore."

Dale looks impish. "What about my asshole?"

I stare at her. I want to be sure here. So I ask, "Have you visited there?"

"Yeah," she says, almost defiantly.

"Okay, then it is another place to explore. But I'll be frank, I think ass-play is a very tricky part of the sexual mix, especially between men and women. I believe anuses are loaded with power and danger and should only be approached at a higher level. Baca on the other hand…"

"Yeah?"

"Baca is in love with the anus. He calls it the true flower of a woman and he has learned to include it early in the whole mix of sex play. But only with lips and tongue. He makes it fun and loves the whole idea of it."

"So maybe this is something Baca can show me."

"Ooh, listen to you! Maybe it is. I know he would be delighted and treat you respectfully, but again, in my opinion, it can sometimes complicate a clear path to the next level."

❧

EMILIO—

My father is a total fucking lunatic. In some ways, it'd be easier if I knew he was just scamming everybody—some high-level grifter deal. But he's really into this awareness shit, so it gets kind of embarrassing but then I'm like, fuck it, the dude could be selling insurance or working for the Pentagon so I'm down with it. But then Rania brings a girl up here like the one yesterday on the sidewalk, and I'm thinking, that girl, she's my age. And so it kinda kills me, you know, me knocking around Ojai over the weekend, surf flat, no music happening, and he's up there with this beautiful girl and Rania too.

❧

BACA—

My son Emilio has an open invitation to my house. Any time of the day or night. Company or no company. Emilio has the key.

ॐ

DALE—

I'm sitting alongside Baca in his Volvo, gliding down Foothill Road, and I'm feeling really fucking good. Whatever they've been putting me through, at this point, it's totally working. Baca's driving through side streets, because it's Saturday afternoon and the main drag is jammed with tourists. Fucking tourists. Not like me. I'm an adventurer. I'm here with purpose. No latte and ice cream for me. I'm like a couple days away from being named Ojai Sex Goddess of the Week. Baca looks over and smiles at me, and suddenly it feels like he knows everything I'm thinking—oh, shit. I stare at him. His profile—strong nose, dark skin, piercing eyes, white teeth. His tapered brown fingers on the steering wheel.

For the first time, I want to touch him. I want to touch him and make him feel good. And suddenly he says, "It is important that we are not sexual, yes? It is cleaner that way."

"Yeah?"

"Yeah."

"But what about Rania? She touches me that way."

"Yes, but her touch is light. In fact, one night maybe you sleep with her. Not so to make love, but she is a very good hugger and kisser and for me, I will try and not be jealous."

I stare at Baca.

"You mean, I can't touch you at all? Never?"

"Of course. A hug and a kiss. But we all know that line where it becomes more. And that's a place we cannot go."

"Then how about my asshole?"

Baca's head jerks. He smiles and laughs. "Who told you this? Did Rania tell you this? That woman has a big mouth, yes? A big fucking mouth!" We're both laughing and I shout out,

"No, no! I figured it out. I'm not an idiot, you know."

"I am," says Baca.

℃

RANIA—

I'm at peace with Baca bringing Dale out on the town for an hour. Ordinarily, it is not good for a woman to step out of our cocoon so early in the process. But Dale is tricky, and so I'm following Baca's lead on this one. His intuition. She may need some jostling. She is one to test things before believing in them.

I use the time alone to shower and lotion, then I sit quietly with a magazine and a glass of Vermouth.

℃

EMILIO—

At the bar at the Ojai Beverage Company, and it's dark and cool, and people are into a nice quiet vibe, right? I'm alone with a half-finished glass of wine when I look up the long narrow wine racks that lead to the front door. There she is, the girl from yesterday, with my Pops holding the door for her, peering into the dark bar. I gulp my wine and stand up, thinking about heading out the side door. My old man is always dragging me into shit. But I see her walk in and I decide to stay. She really is gorgeous. My age, maybe a year older or younger than me. And walking into the cool dark, she's carrying that glow that a few

44

hours up on Foothill can give you. She leads my Pops between long racks of wine bottles.

DALE—

So of course I'm thinkin' am I getting set up here or what? But I'm looking at this guy—and he's gotta be like maybe, maybe my age, right? But he looks so fucking healthy. He's tall and lean and bronzed and he's got this unruly head of semi-dreads all blond and brown, and washed out blue eyes and a real mouth and strong jaw. He's wearing a white t-shirt and loose pants, like pajama bottoms almost and flip flops. And I'm thinking if half of him is from Baca, then I'm wondering where the other half came from, who his mother was, and later I learn she was some Swedish Tantrica which is some kinda Tantra sexual thing, and she made a real splash, you know. In certain circles. Fifteen years ago. But now they barely see each other. Emilio smiles at me and God he's handsome, and he's got this cute innocent look 'cause he knows I saw him about to cut out then decide to stay, and so he cops to that just with one look and I'm thinking, I am in tune here. Or he's in tune, and suddenly I'm wondering if my mouth is open, but then thank God Baca comes to life, hugging Emilio, kissing him on the lips, turning to me, "Dale, this is Emilio, Emilio, this is Dale." We smile at each other but don't step together to shake hands. Instead Emilio raises his hands together, like he's praying, and he bows a bit and says, "Namaste," and like some fucking idiot I put my hands together the same way and bow and say, "Back atcha," but there's this sudden jolt of energy between us and it's like my whole being falls into his deep baby blues. We sit on these stools and Baca orders a crisp white Fume-something for me.

BACA—

I do not set this up. Sure I think maybe he is here. But I don't know. People sit in their houses all day and say everything will happen now, now I will find the light and nothing happens. And they wonder why. It is better to get out of the house.

So together we sit and drink wine and we start talking, and Emilio and I start about the EU Championships, how again it is Spain and Italy, and if I am watching, so early on a Sunday morning. But it is easy, no? In front of Dale. A father and son talk football. And then these two young people start talking. It's easy with them too. I see this a lot. Some people say it is too casual, but how can you say this? Two total strangers—at their peak—they meet each other and find the pathways, talking about art and travel. Emilio has been all over the world. Peru of course, but then chasing waves—Hawaii, the South Pacific. Cape Town, Portugal. Dale stares at him as he talks. Until he catches himself. And then my beautiful son, his mother raised him well, he asks what about her. And so she talks of her one big travel. From Ohio to Los Angeles. It is funny and sad. I can see the glow in her. How she is feeding off Emilio and me. The shared energy.

Then Dale starts to talk a bit about her experience so far with Rania and me. I can see Emilio how he leans back, the clear sign not to continue, but Dale is feeling some power now, she is confident and wants to share. Not reading the sign. Before she goes so far, Emilio jumps in, "Hey so I'll see you again, maybe?"

"If they'll let me," says Dale. "Like tonight I mean. I don't know what kind of kinky shit they have in mind for me."

I can see that Dale means to be funny, yes? A little provocative. And maybe she is one that just a little wine is too much. But anyway, Emilio, he stiffens. "Yeah, well, I gotta go. Pops, love you." Emilio and I hug and kiss. Then Emilio says goodbye to Dale and he is out the door and Dale, she's knows she pushed a button there, and she feels bad. She looks at me.

I shrug and say, "Did you say something dishonest?"

"No," she says. "But it was kinda rude. Not thinking."

"Ah," I smile. "Listen, if you make these hard little nuggets in your body every time you mess up, there's no help for you."

"Yeah?"

"Yeah. Let's go across the street and buy a small chicken and greens and a Pinot Noir and go back up Foothill and cook, okay?"

"Okay."

And that's what we do.

❦

EMILIO—

I tell people I don't buy into all my Pops' bullshit, right? But everything that he's got, I got too. You know why? Since I was like seven or eight, after my mom left, and Rania came into our lives, Rania started talking to me. You know, the ebb and flow stuff. The moon and sun. Girls and boys. And I'm really young so I think okay this is Rania just being Rania. There was nothing graphic about it. It was trippy nature talk. Lots about Yin and Yang. And somehow all that became part of me. So, when I'm a teenager, I was way ahead of the game. And now I'm a man. And I'm carrying this energy, this ability to perceive things about people and understand their needs.

Like Dale. The instant I meet her I know where she needs to go before she can move on. For me, it's just instant. I get it. And it's not something she's gonna get from Rania and Baca. They're good at what they do. And I'm not saying that what I've got is all she needs, right? But without it, I think she'll be wandering in circles.

RANIA—

Alone up at Baca's house, and of course I am worried when they are not home by six. The sun is still warm, streaming low through the trees, but they should be home by now. And finally there they are. I'm at the front door. Dale steps from the Volvo and I can see she has gone contemplative. That lonely, uncertain place that all of us slip into when we have missed a beat or have been thrown off balance.

I step up to her and return to our old greeting, a kiss on each cheek, as I whisper, "*Hola, mon petit choux, la vie est tres compliquee, ce n'est pas?*"

"Yeah," she says.

"So go relax. Some time alone."

Dale walks past me and heads for her room. I see how she carries every emotion in her body, those long arms and legs seeking to move in unison but being pulled every which way. Usually her body goes into defiance when things don't go her way. But not now. She walks down the hall. I turn to Baca who's unloading the canvas bag of groceries. He looks at me and shrugs.

"What happened?"

"Emilio."

"Emilio? She met Emilio? You introduced her to Emilio?"

"It's not on me, Rania. It's her. She's bringing him out. At Ojai Beverage. It was actually nice. They like each other. And you know how she is when we leave here. So filled with life. And he loves this. But then she hurts his feelings."

"Oh, no."

"By talking about us. The sex stuff."

"Oh." But then I think about this. "And Emilio has a reaction. Good for him. She should know not to go certain places. She knows you are his father."

"She gets all revved up, this one."

"I know. But, Baca, you taking her out like that…"

"Rania, you gotta go help her out of this. Go make it right."

"Baca."

"I know," he says. "Sorry."

∽

DALE—

It wasn't the thing with Emilio. It was what Baca said afterwards. Like it's so easy to see I'm totally out of joint. I fuck up and it should be nothing but I'm fucking horrified, then that quick I'm like fuck it, it's nothing, but then there's some little gnarly piece of me that starts fusing together between my muscles somewhere, I don't know. And I'm like oh, great, there goes another one. It's where do I start with myself? I'm willing to try to fix things, and I'm up here right? In Ojai? But then I meet Emilio and I'm thinking somewhere, like somewhere deep down in me, that this guy and I could really connect. We could. I can sense this calm strong thing he has, and it's like he's hanging in with me, I don't put him off you know, like a lotta guys, but then I'm suddenly a fucking idiot blabbermouth and start talking about Rania and Baca and the guy's outta there like a shot. And I don't blame him. One more fuck-up on my part.

∽

BACA—

Rania and I are still in the kitchen. And she is still pissed off. "You better cook us an excellent dinner tonight, maestro."

49

She finishes her Vermouth then climbs up the several steps and walks down the long hallway to Dale's room. Whew. Women. I unwrap the naked chicken and go to work. It sometimes seems stupid, because we keep killing animals, but each time I dress a chicken I make a little apology. And then when I am not eating meat I find myself apologizing to the baby spinach. So here I am, a man full of apologies. Eh…

An hour later we sit around the outdoor table, under Chinese lanterns, eating my perfectly cooked chicken and a bowl of greens. Dale is in fine spirits. Rania has worked her magic.

The light is beautiful, the Ojai pink moment as the sun sets, a rising moon, the Chinese lanterns. We are all glowing. It is very physical, yes? The sharing of food and glances and smiles. But it is above that. The three of us feel it together. We are raising up the game. And this is one important thing— like Rania says, Baca, write that down. But it is so simple this then, for human beings, those times you are together, and in harmony, that is the meaning of existence, yes? I look at this girl, then I turn to this woman I know so well. The energy between us, it is heaven. My body, my mind, my heart, my spirit, I am cruising on all cylinders.

Then of course, Rania breaks the spell.

"There is an issue here that must be addressed." I groan. Dale laughs. Rania gives me a look and goes on.

"When people are doing intimate work like this, attachments develop. Desires, transferences of emotions. It is wrong to deny them. But there are boundaries that must be observed."

"Why?" asks Dale.

And this makes me smile. It is good for Rania, when she grows intellectual, that someone asks why.

"Because," she says, "The alternative leads to chaos."

"And that's bad?" says Dale.

"Ask Manny," says Rania, a bit stern. I have no idea what she's talking about but Dale seems to get it. Rania continues.

"But this is an age-old dilemma. Especially for men."

"No!" I shout.

"Hah, Baca. You know. Especially with men, and as they get older, any girl that strolls by, you devour them with your eyes."

"Of course," I say. "You cannot deny the masculine."

RANIA—

I'm amused at Baca's jargon, "Oooh, listen to Baca." He shrugs. It is Baca's honesty that makes these conversations work with women. I turn to Dale, "Men are who they are. You can choose to ignore them, or you can choose to channel their masculine energy and make this work for you."

"But why is it on me?!" Dale erupts. "Really? I'm serious. On us? Women."

Baca and I look to each other. I defer to him and he says, "This is the design we are given. I know nothing except for this."

Dale looks skeptical, but remember, we are filled with vibrancy here, the three of us. The conversation is a dance, a three-way flirtation. I say, "Men desire young vibrant women."

"But that makes everything all fucked up."

"Not really. Then it's a matter of what is done with that energy. We cannot be having sex with every pretty boy or girl we see, even if they would let us. Men must learn this. And women too."

Dale is staring at me, and I look back into this beautiful girl's eyes, and I almost swoon. "See, for you too. I know you've wanted to touch Baca today. To share a physical intimacy with him."

"How do you know that?" Dale asks.

"I could taste it in the air as you left for town."

Dale looks to Baca and back to me and says, "So, yeah, okay? Can you blame me? It's like me and you. And you know what I'm talking about."

And at those words I flush with love and desire for this girl. Oh, God. Oh, no. I'm falling. Right here I know now that it's true. I have fallen in love with Dale. Oh, Jesus. I look to Baca and he has that curious look in his eye—"I know"—and I realize how hopeless this is. I take a moment. I have no choice now but to bury my secret and soldier on, adding a protective layer by deliberately lowering the temperature.

"This is one of the fundamental challenges we face: the attraction to youth and beauty and how to manifest that attraction." I look to Baca. "Baca, tell her."

"Look, it's simple. Pay attention. I see somebody. I feel a sexual desire. I know I cannot act, right? So I breathe her in. Say it is you. And I let you enter inside me, through my breathing and taking you in, and I am at peace with that. That I will never touch you, but I have a secret. You are touching me. I have brought you inside of me. And then I move along my day, la-di-fucking-da you know, but everyone I see, I share you with them. You. I have a smile, okay? A glow now. Because of you."

"Wouldn't you rather just fuck me?" Dale asks.

"Of course he would," I say. "But I won't let him."

Dale laughs, but Baca stares into her eyes. "Do you have a dragon tattoo someplace I didn't notice?"

"Yeah," she answers, "and it really hurt."

We laugh. We have reached a higher place through this crazy talk. And there is an even higher sexual charge now that is bouncing between us. Baca must take some credit for this. The masculine must not cower.

DALE—

All right, so in one way this whole trip is seeming kind of weird, but in this other way, there's all this heat and consciousness going on between us. Like I'm physically feeling this vibe these two are sending out. And now it's late and they walk me down the hall together and I'm feeling, let me try and get this right, I'm feeling sexual, right? But not really sexy. I'm feeling like this higher buzz of sex. I feel it in me, but I'm feeling it between us. It's not all about them. But it's about where they're bringing me, and at the same time, I mean if either of them just reached over and touched my boob, you know, or kissed me, I swear I'd be like let's do this, let's get this motherfucker on.

BACA—

And me, I'm thinking, this girl, no way we go there with her, so I look at Rania like let's get this girl to bed. So that's what we do, walk her to her room. We hug, we kiss. And by now, you know, it's all electricity with high sex between us. Then Rania takes over with those little cooing noises she learned in Lebanon or someplace. Whispering in Arabic and French and Hebrew for Dale to go slow, and pleasure herself tonight. To start on the outside. And I see Rania touch Dale's neck, her ear, and Dale nods yes. And I'm standing there like let's get down the hall already. And finally we say goodnight and are out the door.

એઝ

DALE—

My body has never felt this way. Not in my entire life. And not just my body. My mind has gone into slow motion. I'm in rhythm. And I'm happy to be alone. I don't even think about the day, but as I brush my teeth, I look in the mirror. I look at my face. Not my pussy. My face. And usually, you know, I do this and in thirty seconds I'm crying, but now I stare into my own eyes and I see in deeper. And it feels okay. And I'm glad to be alone.

❧

RANIA—

Baca and me—running down the hall, running. Big smiles, but wordless as he flings open his bedroom door and pulls me inside. Then he closes it with a sharp click of the catch. He takes me into his arms and kisses me. He pulls my body into his, then he says, "I'm just a minute."

And that fast he's into the bathroom and I hear the strong stream of his pee into the toilet and I think, I'm in a heightened state but I'm out of balance here—suddenly awash again in this overpowering rush of love for Dale. I must channel this powerful emotion or I will lose my mind. Channel it through Baca. I must make the adjustment, find the rhythm between us—we are both already so sexually aroused—but this will be subtle now. As he walks out from the bathroom. I know this man. His sexual energy can shift so quickly, turn on a dime. I breathe deeply, knowing that what is to come tonight between Baca and me will be of the moment. Because that is the promise of Baca. And of Dale.

❧

DALE—

Okay I'm alone, and I'm sexed up to a very high level. And the air is warm and it's incredibly quiet and I'm feeling the spirit. I light a candle. I lie back and know that I'm safe. God, how good it feels to be safe like this. My body tingling, my brain half asleep. But when I go to touch myself I decide against it. I keep my hands by my sides and open my body up and close my eyes and just feel my whole body rushing through the day again. And ending up where? At the bar with Emilio.

Emilio. The very thought of him makes my pussy quiver and flush with liquid heat. Just like that. Emilio.

༄

RANIA—

I'm standing against the bed, waiting for Baca to vacate the loo. Wondering who I should be, myself or Dale. Those are the only choices tonight. And if Baca is on his game, then I can be both. I can be Dale. I can be her for him. That's a beautiful challenge for me. And to feel his lust for her is for me to almost steal it from her, because really it is hers, is it not? This role I can play. But when I play myself, and it's Dale that I want, that is the challenge for Baca. He can be Dale, and he knows this but it takes a certain frame of mind. And maybe that's why he's taking so long. But he is powerful, this man. A true shape-shifter.

BACA—

In a moment like this, it's all a swirl, but the thing about having a lover like Rania? She knows me. She knows me deep. So if I go this way or that, she will go with me. Finally I open the door, and I decide to be me, Baca, the man, as we begin and Rania must know to be Dale.

RANIA—

When he steps from the bathroom I feel from him a blast of pure masculine energy. I rush to him and kiss him because that is the way of girls like Dale who are raw and uncertain. I shock Baca for a second, until he understands and then he begins to perform his magic on me. And he is everything that any girl needs. He is gentle and strong. Insistent, but always

55

talking, asking, reassuring. Kissing. Kissing and kissing. He sits me on the edge of the bed, my feet dangling. He stands in front of me and touches my cheek. I am awash in the emotions of Dale—she is so young, so vulnerable. So in need of proper touch and love. Baca's touch and love. I feel overwhelmed by his every gesture, but why does he move so slowly? My hands shoot out to the belt buckle of his jeans but he brushes them away.

"Ssssh," he whispers. "This is for me now, yes? Me undressing you." Then he reaches and unbuttons my shirt, button by button. I feel his knuckles brush against my neck, my breasts at the edge of my lace bra, then as his hands move down, across the small fold of my stomach, brushing against my navel and then just below until the last button is undone and he slips my shirt off my shoulders. I am in a trance now as he leans over me and kisses my neck and reaches to unclasp my bra. My breasts release and Baca glides back and kneels before me and nestles his face between them.

I am Dale, I am a young rose and Baca is slowly peeling back my petals. One by one, with great gentleness and conviction he is exposing me. Finding his way to my rosebud essence and I have no choice but to give it up to him. This is the way to discovery. This is the way to the light. I shudder as he pushes me back on the bed and undoes the drawstring of my pants. He reaches behind me with both hands and slips his fingers into the waistband. I feel the backs of his fingers against my ass, my hips and I'm thinking rip them off me, will you? Yank them down. But he continues to go slow. Finally my pants are off and he tosses them behind him. No folding here. Then he kneels again in front of me and spreads my legs with his strong hands, and he begins talking.

"For me, always. It is when a woman is not totally naked, but wearing her underpants, yes? And for me, to see that and touch that and feel that, that is the best thing. I can touch you,

you see? Get to know you. Through your panties. Feeling the mound. Your hair underneath. And maybe feeling the swell of you..."

Baca is touching me through my panties and I fight to control my breathing, to not get ahead of myself. I could come in a moment but that is not Dale so I resist his touch, and I feel his fingers immediately grow more urgent against my yoni, my puss, my sex.

"I can get to know your *concha* through your panties and it is such a beautiful thing. Some moisture, yes? Coming through. The hardness of your clit. I can feel that with my fingers. I feel it."

Baca suddenly lifts me and delivers my near-naked body fully onto the bed. It is a surprise move and it thrills me. "Baca," I say.

"Shhhh," he answers. I close my eyes. I sense him getting undressed.

Then he's on the bed alongside me. Pressing against me, and I feel his erection pressing into the flesh of my hip and I gasp, realizing I am losing all control. This cannot be. I feel his masculine energy growing so strong I know I am losing my chance to reverse roles. I look for an opening. He has me on my back, him lying alongside, one leg thrown over between mine, head propped up on his left elbow, leaning in on me, the fingers of his right hand gently stroking circles around my breast. It is slow and sensuous because you can feel in Baca the intensity of him. In the moment. Baca in the moment. And when you have that, you have every combination of touch and attitude a woman could ever want.

"I want to touch your yoni," Baca says.

"Go for it," I respond, searching for Dale's voice.

And he does. First slipping off my panties with one deft motion. Gently nudging apart my thighs. Working his way in from the outside, my navel, my thighs, the dips in my abdomen just inside my hip bones. His fingers are sure and easy with me until finally he has closed in on my pussy that so wants the feel of his touch. He works his way up and down each side, teasing, gently tugging, parting. He says, "I lick my fingers now, and find my way inside you. *Con su permiso.*"

"*Si*," I answer. "*Si. Si.*"

And so he does that, spreading my labia and laying one finger along the length of me, not inside yet, but along the length. And it is wet and soft and warm and I realize, aha, this is my chance. My opening to turn the tables.

"You like that?" I ask. "Fingering me like that?"

"Yes," says Baca.

"So let me return the favor," I say, and here suddenly I am channeling Dale all the way, her strong physicality, those long arms and legs fighting for what they want. And now I have Baca turned and on his stomach, and now, as myself, I push apart his legs then plant a firm hand in the middle of his back, and at that moment he becomes Dale, and he knows it and I know it. And I am myself. So I drop the intensity, and push my breasts up along her back and nuzzle into her hair and whisper it's all right. It's safe and good. It's sharing the love and the art. And I can feel her respond, spreading her legs, letting me slip my hand between her milky white thighs.

Baca plays the part so well, kissing me as Dale, tentative, then strident. Kissing my breasts. Taking a nipple into her mouth. I am overcome with love and joy and sex for this young woman. My eyes fill with tears. Baca senses my mood swing and switches roles on me.

So we go back and forth like that, Baca and me. Controlling our breathing. Finding the rhythm of breath as our bodies meld together. Transferring Dale back and forth between us in perfect syncopation. We are dancing very well tonight, but I know we are on the razor's edge.

And now I just want it over. It is scaring me, this dance of love-transferred. My aching for Dale is so real and tender and true. And knowing it is Baca who I am with, I fear it may take some unforeseen psychic toll. But for now, it is good. I feel Baca's male energy overwhelming him and I know we are to finish with me as Dale. It is best this way. For him but also for me. My sudden rush of love for her threw me off balance, and I must now let it go. What better way than to be her for one last moment. To be Dale and give myself up to Baca. "Take me now. Take me." I roll onto my back and spread my legs.

He withholds his penis from me. I grasp for it and it is hard and firm in my hand, but he keeps his hips back and away even as I spread my yoni for him. I touch myself and yearn for the days when I could generate all the wet we needed, but Baca understands and rolls a bit and reaches—me watching his brown torso in the soft light. A squeeze of Aloe Cadabra. He applies it to his cock and my pussy and now I am finally and completely Dale, young Dale, as he whispers to me, "*Le ayudo a saberse. Le vengo con confianza y honor.*" And I spread my legs farther and his fingers are so knowing and so gentle as he kneels in front of me and says,

"Are you ready, baby?"

"I'm ready," I say. My body charged throughout, already in orgasm, but not climaxed yet, and now feeling his energy and need and masculinity. He places his cock at the entrance to my aching yoni, and rubs it beautifully over my clit, through my lips, lingering at my entrance, then back up to my clit, then sliding down again. Over and over until I am mad with the desire to have him inside of me. And this next time, as he moves his cock lower between my labia, I thrust my hips forward and in one quick plunge he is deep within me. We both cry out. Staring into each other's eyes. We lay there still as can be, feeling the deep melding rush of love and sex coursing through our bodies. I have both my hands on his muscular ass, locking him deep within me. We control our breathing, getting it in perfect synchronization, the waves of sex spreading through us, hotter and hotter, flush with heat radiating through my torso, my hips, overwhelming my young pussy in all its glorious parts. "Now," I say. And with three, four, five strong thrusts and his thumb quick on my clit we are both crying out, climaxing together. Wave after wave of orgasmic full-body energy, vibrating, exploding, bursting, squirting with heat and lust and love. Sending me to a place far beyond.

BACA—
Off the charts.

∽

DALE—
Who are these people? I haven't even rung my evening bell yet and it's like man these two are being loud. I thought Manny and his wife upped the volume, but these two. I gotta laugh. And now that it's clear they're finished, I can settle into myself. Feeling this incredible comfort and degree of relaxation that I feel I've never known. It's weird with all the sexual energy that suddenly I can think of nothing but sleep. But then, as I'm drifting off, some little part of my brain starts thinking, did they plan that? Was that for my benefit? You know, because there are all these people running around traumatized because they saw their parents fucking when they were kids maybe, or maybe they only heard it, but that created these blockages, right? So maybe Rania and Baca, it's like they're telling me, okay, listen to us making love. With love. Process this and get over it. Am I crazy here? But they are kinda like parents to me by now. And I just heard them fuck each other's brains out and I feel fine. So one way or the other, it's part of the show I guess.

I fall asleep thinking of Emilio. Emilio, staring into my eyes. Touching my cheek with his fingertips. What did Rania say? Start at the beginning.

ᘓ

RANIA—

We are sleeping. I hear a key throw the bolt of the front door. My eyes open in the dark. I grope with my hand and find Baca's thigh and hip. He stirs. I lie thinking, who is this now in our house, and then it comes to me, and my body relaxes and sinks back into the mattress.

ᘓ

DALE—

Okay so check out this dream I have. I wake up to a strange sound. I am very very sleepy. I hear the faint drone of a TV. And then voices. Men's voices. I climb out of bed, wearing my beautiful cotton nightgown. I open my door and look down the dark hall. At the far end, down a half set of stairs into the living room I see a blue glow. It's the TV. I slowly walk down the long hallway until I reach the top of several steps and look down onto the scene. The TV is on some soccer game. Baca sits in a chair in a robe, his feet up. And on the sofa, Emilio. From the back his hair is wild and messy. Their eyes are on the screen, as if they were one creature. They are really into this game.

I walk down the stairs. They look up at me together and smile then return to the game. Then Emilio pats the cushion alongside him on the sofa and says, *"Siéntate aqui conmigo."*

And I do. I sit next to him and I pull my bare feet up and I lean my head against his shoulder and we watch soccer in the dark. And all I can remember is me thinking, hold this moment, don't fall back asleep, as I feel this magnetic pulse of

61

masculine energy between the game and Baca and Emilio. And then a goal, and they're excited, leaping up. And when Emilio sits back down, he wraps his arm around me and pulls me closer against him, my head nestled under his armpit, pressed against his strong lean rib cage. I feel the gentle swell of his breathing. His strong arm draped over my shoulder and down my side, his fingers idly stroking my hip, my thigh through the soft cotton nightgown. I can smell him.

It is a dream. I know this. I wake up alone on the living room couch, a blanket thrown over me. The sun just coming through the windows. On the floor, below me, a rose in a plastic water bottle. I stare and smell and smile and drift back to sleep.

❧

RANIA—

It is dawn. The first morning rays stream through the pepper trees. I sit quietly at the outdoor table, trying to get a handle on myself. I focus on my breathing. I sip tea. I cry. But the huge mix of emotions overwhelms me this morning. Why does love hurt so much, and why does this hurt turn into a lacerating anger? An anger I must turn on someone else or it will slice my insides to a bloody mess. Oh, God. Welcome to womanhood. It never ends, does it? No matter the work we put in. It never ends.

So I sit here, spine straight, waiting for Crouching Yoda and Sleeping Beauty to awaken. Just the thought of her, Dale, still asleep on the couch, her breath gentle, dreaming God knows what after her little trip through fairy land with Baca and Emilio. It made me crazy as I lie sleepless in bed, listening to the electronic drone of the television—two tribes of sweaty men striking a ball with their heads and their feet, their hands forbidden. What? What am I talking about? I am all over the place this morning. But think about it—their hands tied.

Football, soccer, I see how really it is an elevated sport. For men to make sport without using their hands.

Fucking men.

And fucking Dale.

This morning she will get hers from me. She needs to feel others' pain. The way she throws her weight around. So reckless. I am tired of being the understanding one. I am tired of playing Mother. And so I will show my hurt in front of her. I will teach her a lesson. I will. Just you watch.

ᘒ

BACA—

I wake up and that fast I am thinking oh, boy, this will be some morning here. I want to roll over and enter again the dream of Dale, snuggled on the couch. I can smell her hair and the sweet sting of the sweat from her armpits. I was surprised yesterday in the studio to see that she even shaves there. But this girl to me, she is not a body, she is a force. A force that is about to run headfirst into Rania. And me, wanting only to roll over. But I cannot. I need to be there. I can feel Rania's black energy. I must prepare myself. So first a shower, strong coffee, and a nice clean dump in the privacy of my own bathroom.

ᘒ

DALE—

I roll from the couch. I lean over and smell the rose. I am filled with joy and light and love and I'm thinking, what the fuck is this? This isn't like me. I can't wait to see Rania this morning. Her beauty, her calm. I just want to hug her and thank her. And maybe promise to stop cussing so much.

RANIA—

Baca has the balls to join me first. I could bite his head off. I could slap him silly. But he has this way of deflecting me. Maybe because he is Latin, and also somewhat enlightened. He knows to keep his mouth shut and offer a plate of mango and watermelon with a conciliatory shrug. He sits and says nothing, and then suddenly she is there, in the doorway, still in her nightgown, rubbing the sleep from her eyes.

"Good morning," she says. "Can I tell you guys something?"

Baca looks to me. This time it is me who shrugs. Baca nods at her.

"I feel beautiful," Dale says as her eyes fill with joy and tears.

Baca smiles, but I do not. I stare at her, cool, sullen. She shrugs me off, that is her power. That's the street in her. She turns to Baca and they flirt about how she wants more bodywork and what exactly was that late last night. The soccer game. She is trying to understand the visit. As I stare, my longing for her grows deeper and stronger by the moment. I am speechless for how stupid I am being. Idiot. *Idiota. Sazalra.* I've been with other women of course. I was never one to deny myself pleasure. But for me it was more cuddle and less raw sex. And to fall asleep in a woman's arms, that is bliss. But now, here, with Dale, I feel lust. I want to kiss her deeply. Press our bodies together. Melt into each others' arms. I want to love her and I want her to love me back. I do. I want to make her hot and suckle her breasts and feel the wet of her pussy when my fingers finally reach there. But this is crazy. Where did this come from? She is beautiful. I smell her. I can taste her. I want to have her and for this I know I will pay a deep deep price.

I listen to their playful banter as Dale asks, "Did you guys like drug me last night or something? I'm talking Emilio."

"Yes," Baca answers.

"But he was there. On the couch."

"Yes. You see, I know Emilio very well. He is my son."

"Yeah, well, so how come he split?"

"You were asleep," says Baca. "It was best."

Dale simply smiles. But I've got a bee in my bonnet.

"He's playing games with you," I tell Dale. "When we are asleep is when we are most suggestible." I stare into her eyes and say, "Have you read Gaston Bachelard?" And with that simple question Baca shoots me a sharp look. Of course she hasn't. She hasn't read anything. She's a blank slate this girl, and it's wrong of me to take a dig like that. But she knows nothing. Nothing of literature, politics. The Greeks. Eastern philosophies. She knows nothing. Nothing but the streets. Plus she knows how to draw a true line. And how to get a rise out of me.

"Who?"

"A French philosopher," I say. "He warned that while sleep is so necessary for the body, it also opens the soul to phantoms."

"No shit," says Dale. "I've had nightmares like from when I was a kid. Like forever."

"I'm not talking about the obvious. I'm talking about phantoms. Phantoms over whom you have no control."

Dale stares at me curiously then tries a smile that I don't return so she turns to Baca. "What is she talking about?"

Baca answers, "Beats me. Guess you gotta read the book."

And that fast the rage comes roaring back through me. I take a deep breath and with a tight smile I stand and go inside.

⁊

DALE—

Oh, man. I'm in the back seat of Baca's Volvo. Baca's driving and Rania's shotgun. We're supposed to be heading off to hear this talk on top of some mountain or something, but with these two and how fucking tense they are now, I'm wondering if we don't end up in a ditch. We're driving down this long straight road and Baca's driving really slow. Like really slow and I can feel Rania's energy just banging around inside the car, like he's doing it on purpose, and I'm sitting in the back seat thinking, man, you're bringing me back to Ohio with this shit, and then Rania says to him,

"So you want us to be late?"

"Late to what? To hear one more talk by one more enlightened one who will only tell us we are late for a reason, no?"

"So you deride all this, so don't go," says Rania.

"Maybe I won't."

"So don't. Okay? You can drop us off there and leave." Baca says nothing so Rania jumps back at him, "You tell me then, how do you want this day to go?"

"How can I answer? You bring this strange girl into my house. Everything upside down. And then you…"

"Baca, she's in the back seat!"

"Hello," I shout. "Remember me?"

"I know she's in the back seat," says Baca, and then he adjusts his mirror and we're eyeballing each other. "Hey, uh, Dale, Dale, you want I should leave you out of this?"

And I'm thinking, hey, he actually got my name right, and I say, "No way."

"So don't mind us, okay? We are on edge, yes? Rania and me. *Como agua para chocolate.*" And something about the Spanish, me not understanding a word of it, but the roll of it, it suddenly makes the whole car go easy. Baca's eyes moving from me in the mirror to the road to Rania. And then he says, "Rania, at least it keeps the sex fresh, yes? Yes?" Rania eyeballs him as Baca says, "Don't lie in front of this girl. Look at her and tell her the truth."

Rania softens a touch and turns to look at me. Her eyes are so deep and beautiful I can't even tell what color they are. "So yes," she says to me. "It keeps the sex fresh. But is it worth it? We aren't even married and we squabble like this! Baca, you shit, we aren't even married!"

"And whose fault is that?" he says.

Whoa. Wrong thing to say.

Rania goes all stiff again. It's like Raging Hormones as she glares at him.

Baca tries to deflect it, "My fault of course. It is all my fault. I'm a witch. I'm a male witch, and it's all my fault."

And here I'm thinking what the fuck is he talking about? But Rania she's all over it. "You're not a witch. You're just lazy and stupid."

And Baca gets this shit-eating grin spreading across his Peruvian face and he's like, "Yeah? That's what male witches are! So, hah!"

"I'm getting out," says Rania. "At the market."

❧

BACA—

She got me. How did this happen? *Merde.* Suddenly I am steering the Volvo down Aliso towards the farmers' market, a gathering, a quiet celebration that I always enjoy but she is the one getting out, yes? Rania is getting out to go walk among friendly souls while it's me going off to this lecture I have heard a thousand times. She gives me her happiest smile and I know she planned this all along. "You two have fun," she tells us.

"Rania, listen," I say. "So maybe at least you could buy us some small potatoes. A yellow onion maybe?"

"Maybe."

"And from Harry's Berries, some strawberries."

"Maybe."

"But you don't have a bag."

"I don't have any money either."

And like that she turns and is gone into the crowd. And now I have some cars trying to creep around me and I know I'm blocking things, but everyone is so polite I think, okay, I'll get moving, but instead I look in the mirror and I say, "So, Dale, are you going to sit in the back like some princess or come up and sit with me?"

DALE—

I was bummed. I wanted to be with Rania walking around the market. Then, the minute I got out and climbed into the front seat and slammed the door the whole vibe changes. This deep wave of warmth and energy comes sweeping into me. It's coming from Baca. It pushes me back into the seat and I feel the sun on me, the heat, and it takes my breath away. Baca pulls out and says, "Dale, breathe with me." And it's like now that he really knows my name, he's using it every time he says something, but I like it. And I close my eyes and I hear him begin to take a deep slow breath and I try to match him, and I can feel my energy moving into him as his moves into mine and we begin to exhale and Baca blows a stop sign and hangs a right as we're exhaling and suddenly I'm thinking hey, don't crash the fucking car here when he's suddenly blowing another stop sign hanging a tricky left onto the main drag and it's busy, you know, there are cars and people and dogs and all sorts of shit, but it like opens for us and we're through and we're safe.

I take another deep breath and say, "What the fuck, man? Did you just blow through two stop signs?"

"What? No. Of course not. I am the safest driver in the world."

⁊

RANIA—

Thank God I am rid of them. My spirits lift. At the farmers' market I am among old friends. I stop and chat, hug and admire. The gray hair, the paunches. The vibrant young adults with their lean relaxed bodies. Then the babies, toddlers, young children turned to towering teenagers, as if overnight. It is all of a piece.

As I glide through the crowd, I am reminded that magic is a quiet thing.

I also know the vendors, the farmers, and I suddenly want to buy, and being the Lebanese that I am, I slip off a shoe and a fifty dollar bill is there and from the first vendor, the offer of a canvas bag. I buy small white potatoes, and a yellow onion, and then scallions, and bib lettuce, and strawberries, as I smell and taste the bounty, feel my sisters and brothers moving in harmony on this sunny Sunday morning in Ojai, California.

⁊

DALE—

I'm expecting some like totally outside mountaintop thing okay, like really rocky and big pine trees, but as Baca drives along and we're suddenly winding up this perfectly paved road I'm thinking okay, whatever. This is not what I thought it was. Not the first time I heard something wrong.

"What is this?" I ask.

"Meditation Mount. Handicapped accessible."

"What does that mean?"

"I don't know. Just something stupid. It's good, actually. It's a good place."

So we reach the top and there's this parking lot up there and it's filled with Volvos and Priuses and old vans with surfboards and bicycles on top, and there's this building, kind of like a pavilion I guess, and everyone is nice, but it's all like quiet in this strange way, like hush-hush, and so I'm thinking okay I'll go with the flow here. Me and Baca, we flow inside, and everyone's smiling and nodding hello to him, but it's crowded. He leads me to a mat on the floor and I sit down and he says, "Dale, I find a seat in the back. My knees you know." And he's gone and I'm sitting in the middle of all these spiritual types and I'm like, hey it's all right like two or three at a time, but I don't know, man. This group thing, I don't know. But it's not like I'm gonna get mugged right? Like some spiritual mugging or something.

BACA—

I find a seat in the back, and I know why I'm really here, why I have brought Dale here, but I do not admit it to myself. No, I say I am here because of William and how he makes me laugh. William is an old man who opens and closes every talk. He is bald and bent like the old man you might find at a bowling alley, renting the shoes. He walks onto the small stage and looks us over. There is a sound in the room. A ripple of knowing laughter. William is very stern. Staring at us like we have smelly socks. Then suddenly his wrinkled face opens up. A big smile. A big big smile. He is missing teeth. We all smile back. We laugh together.

"Stand up," says William.

So we all stand up. We have no power to do otherwise.

"Raise your right hand to the heavens, drop your left hand to the earth."

We do as we are told, and as I peek through the crowd, I see that Dale too has obeyed.

"Know this," says William. "Energy flows from the heavens into this earth and then back again. If you feel it, you will know what I mean. Now close your eyes and feel it."

So of course we all close our eyes and we feel it. And William says, tell me you feel it, and we answer as one we feel it and then he's saying tell me louder and we're saying we feel it, and he brings us up even stronger and louder, just to that right place where it's not too much, you know, like too preacher-like, then he quiets it down and he's done. "Sit," he says. We do and he walks off.

EMILIO—

I'm late to Meditation Mount, but that's what I love about this path, it's like whatever happens was meant to happen. Anyway, I get there and now I'm hanging outside the open doors hearing William do his thing, and I catch a glimpse of my Pops, and I'm wondering if I'm even going in because the surf's decent at county line, and my friends were talking maybe Tony's Pizza after, or beers and halibut sandwiches at Duke's, but I know why I'm here. I spot her. Dale. Right in the middle of everybody, sitting on a mat on the floor, and she's totally quiet and still, and she looks like she's digging it. I decide to hang in.

DALE—

William was cool, but now there's some I don't know Hindu guy up on stage, sitting cross-legged and talking in like this total fucking drone, you know what I mean, and he's talking about sexual magic and sexual mysticism and Tantra and chakras and all this very interesting shit I guess, but it's that fucking drone in his voice like okay so you had an orgasm eating your Cheerios this morning, BFD, I don't know. My ass hurts. My shoulders ache. Then suddenly it all changes. I can feel an electric charge start in my crotch and start spreading all through my body. I feel blood rushing. I feel dizzy. I know he's here. Emilio. I feel his eyes on me. And suddenly I'm paying attention to this swami guy—no disrespect. His words:

"With love and practice you may reach spiritual heights through various methods of sexual intercourse. This we know. This is mystic sex. Also with love and practice you may capture your sexual energy and use it in your everyday life. This we know. This is sex as magic. People may become all backwards with these principles. Sexual energy is to be used for the highest purpose, but also for the most mundane. When you learn to consciously harness this sexual energy, you will be at a great advantage in the game of life."

And on and on he went like that, and I was getting it, you know. I was feeling it. But then it started slipping away. And I knew he was gone. Emilio. I could feel it and I wanted to be out of there. I'd heard enough.

BACA—

I slip out before Dale and stand off to the side, out of view. I know that Emilio is still present. I want to see what he is up to, no? The crowd filters out. I am in no mood to talk and my friends ignore me. Then there she is, Dale, strolling out, spacey, looking for me. I see Emilio, leaning against the building. He spots her and strides quickly forward, and I see how he takes her hand and she cannot resist, simply cannot resist and he knows this and he leads her from the crowd and down a wood chip path, where things are quieter.

I follow. Wondering.

Do you truly appreciate how handsome my son is? He is tall and broad-shouldered. Arms strong from surfing, legs from hiking and climbing. He has an ease and grace. His hair at present is long and unruly, filled with sun streaks, falling into his eyes until he sweeps it back. His skin is both fair and brown, following his mother and me equally. His eyes a strange milky blue, as if he is developing cataracts almost. His mother said his eyes are like that to protect his soul.

The path continues, level, as the young couple strolls hand in hand out along the ridgeline, overlooking the valley—a sweep of groves below us—oranges, avocados, pixie tangerines. The mountains to the north are stark and solid. The little town a few miles to the west. They used this valley as Shangri-La you know. The movie people, Frank Capra, in the 30's, for "Lost Horizon."

EMILIO—

What are you gonna do? A girl like this? My heart is open and true and I am captivated by her. She is leaving tonight and I can't let her. I lace my fingers through hers and pull her to an overlook and point to my right, "You see that mountain with the rock face? Chief's Peak." She turns to look and as she does I curl an arm around her back and I lean in on her and steal a kiss. She doesn't resist so I let my lips linger on hers. She doesn't open her mouth to me, but she doesn't pull away either. I gently press my body against hers until she finally pulls her lips from mine.

"You're a thief," she says.

"I am," I say. She stares at me. "I've wanted to kiss you for as long as I've lived."

"Kiss me again."

DALE—

What? What did I just say? Kiss me again? But as he leans forward I'm glad I said it because now it's a more serious kiss and I open my mouth to his and he tastes of licorice and salt and his lips are full and strong and I feel the blood rushing all throughout my body, everywhere, and suddenly I'm fucking swooning, okay? I'm losing it here, my knees buckling, but his arm is strong against my back, holding me up, and he laughs, pulling his mouth away from mine, staring into my eyes with that Milky Way look, and I feel the beautiful innocence of this guy, this delight he has right now. Like I am the only woman in the world. And I am. I am. But then his eyes grow serious. He loses his smile.

"You're not leaving tonight," he says. "Stay. Stay the week. Rania will drive back for you next weekend."

"Stay with your father?"

"He'd love it. You know how he is. It'll be good for you. And if it feels too tricky, I'll come rescue you."

"Will you?"

"Yes. If you promise to kiss me again."

He smiles and lets me go. "I gotta run. I'm late. You can find your way back?"

"To where?"

"The parking lot."

What's he talking about? "It's right there," I say. I look back and can see the roof of the pavilion.

"I know. But this path we just took, it's not so straight and narrow."

I laugh. "You like fucking with people, don't you?"

He laughs. "Just like my old man, huh?" He reaches and touches my face then he spins and runs up the wood chip path. As I watch him I know that I want him. I want the whole thing. I want the talk and the walk. I'll match him. I will. I've got some seriously impressive shit going on and I don't talk about it too much but I am the shit. And I can walk this walk with Emilio.

I want his baby. How crazy is that? But to me, right now? That's not crazier than anything else in this life of mine.

RANIA—

I'm walking up Foothill Road my bag filled with vegetables and strawberries and a melon and suddenly this isn't such a good idea since the sun is hot and I must keep switching the bag from arm to arm to avoid throwing my back out but of course this will only mean throwing out both sides. I do not hitchhike, but count always on someone offering me a ride. But not today. I feel the sweat suddenly break through my pores, all at once. I laugh to myself. There hasn't been a single thought of my newfound love and lust for Dale. So maybe this is the answer to unrequited love. Break a sweat. But then again, I just thought of her. *Stupido.* I stop to catch my rhythm and there's the Volvo, chugging up Foothill and my heart leaps. Baca and Dale. He pulls over, and I climb wordless into the back seat.

Baca drives. Dale strangely quiet while he and I feel out each other's mood. Dale leaning back, her eyes closed, lost in thought. And as we drive up the long straight road, slowly, without a word, we all start smiling, even Dale, like the Cheshire cat, the loins of her mind still wrapped around Emilio. And then, suddenly Dale is laughing, and Baca too, and finally me, because what is the alternative?

We laugh and laugh and finally we quiet down. Baca says,

"So here we are, the three amigos."

"The three blind mice."

"The three little pigs."

We turn into the drive.

EMILIO—

I knew she was trouble. And when you're attracted to that, what's that say about you? And I knew the answer before the question—because a woman like Dale gives more than she takes. Without even meaning to. Plus I like adventure.

I head back to my cottage on Mallory Way, feeling all stirred up. I have a couple hits of pot and decide what to do. Surf's flat. I consider heading up there to Pops' tonight. Just showing up in the middle of dinner. Then I decide against it—'cause my father, when I challenge him like that, especially with Rania there, he can go very uncomfortable when he thinks I'm not being polite. He can really make things miserable without saying a word. So I kick back and daydream. And make a plan.

☙

BACA—

We are in the kitchen of my house where Rania has taken over, chopping, mincing, rinsing, shredding. "This kitchen is mine now, out. Out."

Dale and I look to each other. "Show me your paintings," she says.

Rania jumps in, "Yes, Baca, go show her your paintings."

So I take Dale's hand and lead her out the door to the studio as Rania calls after us, "And keep your clothes on!"

We walk up the path, hand in hand, and really this is our first true mutual touch, and it is only due to her encounter with Emilio that I take on the father energy. She likes it. I feel it freeing her to enjoy me.

My heart shrugs.

I slide open the doors and walk to my largest canvas. And then, without time to grow anxious, to cringe before this fine young artist who I know will give me her uncensored reaction, yes? I lift the canvas and turn it around.

DALE—

I didn't know what to expect. Nudes? Abstract? So I stared at this canvas and tried to understand. I stared and stared. Finally I said, "You have to show this."

"I can't," he said. "I'll get killed."

I keep staring. It's an intricate construction of white lines on a deep blue-black canvas. Interlocking geometric shapes, I don't know what to call them, you know like hexagons and that stuff, but it's got depth, it's like in 3-D almost and as I keep staring at it my eyes start swimming and I'm feeling embraced by this feeling of connectedness, like this buzzing filling my body and this incredible peace coming over me. Tears come to my eyes. "Baca."

"It's a trick," he says.

"What do you mean?"

"It's a geometric trick. Fractals, they're called. But here, somehow I learned if you bend each line just enough it takes on energy. And somehow that energy, depending on how your brain works, it will trigger dreams."

"Jeez."

"But it's a bitch," he says. "I mean technically, this is a bitch. How do you perfectly bend a line with paint? Free hand?"

"God, I don't know," I say. "I'm a slob with paint. I'm all slob style."

"And for you, that works. But me, for this, what? How will I be judged? A trickster artist. Maybe I should do them on black velvet?"

I keep staring at Baca's painting and I'm getting lost in these very realistic dreams, like hyper-real. Dreams from just last night. I want to just go there, to fall into them, but suddenly I want to turn away. I barely hear his voice say, "You don't want to stare at it too long."

He spins me around and smiles. I'm dizzy. "How does that work?" I ask.

"I don't know. I think sometimes it's the power of suggestion. Sometimes maybe just a trick of Moebius and single plane geometry. I mean how do I show something like that? I'll have people suing me."

I stare at this guy. This Peruvian painter healer guy with the hot son and Rania who is fantastic in every way, and I'm thinking why couldn't you just give me some nudes, man? Give me some hot nudes, but no, he's gotta lay this painting on me, and I feel a little scared. I gotta admit it. I mean who can paint a picture that brings back your dreams?

I ask him, "Does Rania know about this?"

"Of course."

"And what does she say?"

"She tells me let's have a big fire and burn them all up."

On the path, walking back to the house, I have my arm around him and now I'm to the moon about this guy. And it's this weird mix of dad and teacher and just this guy I trust, you know. And this guy who scares the shit out of me.

Then I ask him if I can stay, and he says maybe. That he'll decide over dinner, and that he'll be the one to tell Rania if the answer is yes. Then he warns me, "Dale, she falls in love with you. Rania."

"It's not like that," I say. "It's puppy love. You know."

Baca stares at me. "Rania is many things, but she is no puppy."

❧

78

RANIA—

I stand at the kitchen counter, preparing our meal, the light of the setting sun filtering through the windows, but I am not at peace. I can think of only one thing—Emilio and Dale at Meditation Mount this morning.

Baca is enough to deal with, but Emilio? I feel a pain in my heart, and I immediately tell myself to stop it. Cut it out. I'm giving this girl too much power over me. Whatever is to come, it is not by succumbing. So I buck up. I know how to do this. And tonight, at dinner, she and I will bring out even more of each other, but on equal terms, and on the drive home, with God's blessing, she will fall in love with me.

❧

BACA—

On most June nights, you can feel the marine layer creeping up the Ventura river valley, and even if it doesn't reach us, the chill will be there, so tonight we eat inside, before a fire in the stone fireplace. Rania has cooked us a beautiful dinner—a red vegetable curry, a handful of leaves of Romaine with a touch of olive oil. My contribution, a small jug of young Cabernet from Casa Barranca winery just down the road. The workers bring it to me because we can speak Spanish and I am respectful of them.

Tonight, Rania is radiant. My love. The love of my life. My heart aches for her heart. Her heart so under the spell of Dale. But she serves our dinner and casts a spell of her own. We dig into the delicious curry, savoring the scent, the steam, the bite of the still-young red wine. Rania has made this table and she rules it.

"Sometimes I get so sick of it," she says with a smile. "All this seeking of higher consciousness. Baca, you get sick of it too."

"I just get stuck, that's all."

"But really, Dale are you with me on this? Don't you feel sometimes that this whole quest is so stupid?"

Dale smiles and shrugs. "As opposed to the quest of keeping Manny's asshole friends out of my apartment?"

Rania laughs. "Hey, no more picking on Manny! But I'm serious here. All this quest for the holy. I mean, say you believe in some kind of afterlife, so why not just wait until you die and figure it out then? Why not just recognize that the real miracle is this—of being flesh and blood on planet earth. With all our crazy urges, the lust, the jealousies, the absurd need to prove one's worth just for the sake of it? To show off? Baca, you're getting this, yes?"

And I say, "Of course. Sometimes I think what's the point? All those seekers, spending so much time seeking a higher plane. Denying the earth."

Rania jumping back in, "God, I think of all those hours I spent meditating. All those books and lectures..."

I interrupt, "You spend all this time trying to float above experience, to deny experience, and then you die, okay? But your soul is still awake."

Rania says, "Exactly, exactly. And you find yourself exactly where you wanted to be. In this nice quiet soulful place, and you look around and there are all these other soulful types, and it is oh so elevated."

"Way above the muck and shit."

"And looking down you suddenly realize, oh my God, this is boring up here. I mean, boring."

Dale jumps in, shouting, "Bor-ing. Bor-ing."

"And who knows for sure," Rania continues. "This is the great mystery, but what if you die and get to the other side and you look back and realize that this?—all that we have right now? This is it! Look at us! This, the muck and turmoil, the sex and violence of our existence, that this is heaven."

I add, "And don't forget bliss."

"Yes, bliss too. That it is this. We are here. Heaven. And maybe, once we die, we can never return… We are banished forever."

Then that fast, Rania goes blue. I've seen her crash like this again and again. Suddenly distant, wistful, and I know that she knows Dale is staying. And now I must break the news to her.

"Rania, Dale has decided to spend the week here. You of course are invited as well."

Rania's face does not change. She does not look at me or at Dale. She stares into the fire and it is at moments like this that I love her more than is possible.

☙

DALE—

I walk Rania out to her Mercedes, carrying her bag. The pink sky has gone this beautiful violet color. There's the smell of jasmine or something. Flowers in the cool air. I'm crying. I feel her hurt and I'm crying. I want to hold her. I'm taller so I put her bag in the back seat, then lean against her car and pull her towards me. I pull her body into mine and I feel a charge of love and sex. It feels like the sex I used to have, in a rush, a jolt, you know. And I kiss her. I kiss her with depth of field, you know, with this intensity and she kisses me back, and it's fierce, right? Then we break apart and she says,

"What do you want?"

I don't know what to say. "I, I want…"

"Do you deserve it?"

I don't have to think about this, "Fuck yes."

"Then it's yours, Dale. Claim it. It's yours."

I stare at her face in the fading light. "What about you, Rania? What do you want?"

"You."

"You shouldn't lay that on me."

"I know."

"I love you, Rania. You know that. You're the most important person in my life and I love you for that." And I suddenly like lurch forward and kiss her again, and we're matching each other, lips and tongues, fierce, desperate, but then I feel her soften it. Just a touch—she softens her kiss, and I know it's an invitation. It's a plea. And I cannot go there. Not with her.

"It's Emilio, isn't it?" she asks.

"Rania…"

❧

RANIA—

It is the hardest drive this night. With this ache in my heart and the sting of tears, I know I must drive away. As I pull out, I breathe Dale into me, down through my spine, pushing her down, down through my leg—my thigh, my calf, and into my foot and it is Dale who pushes down on the accelerator. It is Dale who is driving me away.

Down the 33, merging onto the 101, feeling the flow, the flow of humanity in our little metal boxes equipped with rubber wheels, driving to arrive at some other answer.

❧

BACA—

It was sad, yes? This is the worst I have ever seen Rania fall for someone. And with so little hope. It worried me. It was not like her. And now I have this Dale on my hands. There is something Rania whispered to me, just before she left. She said, Baca, this one is dangerous. You be careful. And I said me be careful and not you? But I'm leaving, she said and she was right.

Dale walks back into the house and she's been crying, yes? Her cheeks are wet and on her upper lip a dribble of snot maybe, and we hug in the hallway and I say to her, "I'm going to bed."

"Yeah. And Baca, tonight, please don't come bouncing into my dreams, okay? I don't think I can take it."

"I'll do my best."

~

EMILIO—

I know she stayed. I start to smile but then I catch myself. What the fuck are you doing here, man? What the fuck are you doing? I think about it. About my situation. How maybe it's best that I'm without a partner. Still, I know that I am incomplete, and I know that at least she and I will be good for each other. Even in passing. I'll be up early. If there's surf I'll run down for a few hours. If not I'll roll over. Knowing, she'll be there, at my Pop's as he does his holistic thing with her.

But she's mine.

Dale.

I want her and I'm having her.

~

DALE—

I slept and I woke up with the sun on my face. That's three mornings in a row that I'm waking up feeling good. I remember I'm alone in the house with Baca so I lose the nightgown and put on my clothes and walk down to the kitchen to find him making breakfast and I'm feeling all chipper and I smile and say, "Good morning,"

"Good morning," he says with a smile and he opens his arms and I walk into them and we hug and he says, "Kiss me on the lips. Lightly though."

So I do, and it's nice, no tongue, and he says, "See! It can be like that, yes? I have taken off all the pressure."

"That's uh, really swell."

Baca smiles. "You're a funny one. You know you're really messed up, right?"

"I know that. Thanks for reminding me."

"It's just better to recognize it. I'm not going to bullshit with you. If you want to do some work with me, then okay."

"What kind of work?"

"So you're interested?"

"Yes."

"Okay, then. But first I make you an omelet."

❦

BACA—

So now we're in the studio. Dale and me. And it is the most exquisite feeling, to have a girl like this is my care. I am suddenly feeling holy almost, I know it sounds stupid but after all the push and pull, this girl is a sensitive soul here. I am feeling a duty. To do my best with her.

She wanders around, then smiles in that kind of loopy way and says, "So, Maestro, what's the plan?"

"First I want to draw you. Just 15 minutes. Just to get to know you."

"Naked, right?"

"No, no. A simple portrait. So find a seat someplace, get comfortable."

She looks around then finds a patch of sunlight on the bamboo floor. She sits down and leans up against the white wall. She has aesthetic sense, this crazy girl. Every decision, she shows sense.

I grab my sketch book and a piece of charcoal. I sit on a small chair with wheels and glide my way into position, ending with a little spin that makes her smile. Then I look at her. And I look and look. I take her in. The way every woman deserves to be looked at—like a night sky. The enormous expanse of it. The expanse of her. I look and look. Until a tear rolls down her cheek. And I finally put my charcoal to the paper.

DALE—

This sucks. Having Baca stare at me like this. Fuck, and now I'm crying, well, fuck it, what else can I do? Until he says,

"Hey, blubber-face, cut it out, huh? No crying. Catch your breath."

So I do, and I wipe my face and I thank God I'm not sniffling like usual, and I slowly relax into this moment, hearing the charcoal in his hand scrape against the paper. Quick strokes. And I feel this immense sense of relief suddenly, letting go, letting go of it, letting this man see into me. Draw me. Draw me. Then, suddenly, he's done.

"Here, check it out," he says. "Not bad, huh?"

I stand up and walk over. I burst into tears at this simple sketch. I mean, it's personal, you know, of course. And it's technically just so fine and sure, every mark. But then there's more, like somehow he's capturing a soul here. My soul. He's drawn someone I'd like to know better. "That's who I want to be," I whisper.

"Yeah. But it can be a long way from here to there."

"What's that mean?"

"Nothing. Just some swami bullshit."

"So what's next?"

Baca spins around in his chair a few times. I return to my seat on the floor in the sun.

"We should do some work with symbols. Get you grounded. You need to create a symbol. A representation of yourself. A symbol you can see, yes? In your mind's eye, that will return you to your essence."

"You want me to draw something?"

"Sure, or paint it. It should be simple—it should be like a logo. Your own personal logo. It might seem crazy, but this is a practical trick to return yourself to balance."

"You're full of tricks."

"Yeah, sometimes it's better not to get too deep about this stuff."

Baca flips the page on his sketchbook, walks over and hands it to me, and then the piece of charcoal, then strolls across the studio to look out. I stare at the blank page. It feels good to have charcoal in my hands. I stare and stare. I close my eyes and try to conjure. But nothing comes. "Hey, Swami, I'm stuck."

Baca turns. "Okay. Then close your eyes and picture your navel. Your first physical attachment to this place. To your mother."

I do what he says, just being technical, you know? Like trying to remember what does it even look like?

"Okay, now open your eyes and draw it."

So I start, and it's murky, swirls of black and grey and suddenly I'm getting lost in it, and I'm overwhelmed with emotion that's so fucking raw, seeing my mother, feeling this incredible sense of loss. None of it worked for me. None of it. My whole fucking life. And now I'm sobbing suddenly, and I'm like, "Fuck you, Baca! Fuck you!" I fling the sketchpad at him, send the charcoal skittering across the floor.

He's quiet as I sob. He goes to collect the sketchpad. He looks at my sketch then flips it over the spiral of the pad. He picks up the charcoal then he brings them both back to me.

"Okay, now draw your symbol. Right now. Without thinking. Draw it!"

BACA—

With the charcoal on paper, she draws a perfect circle. Perfect. Then she slashes a bold line right through it, and the circle and line clash with tension and attraction.

Dale is crying again. I'm sitting on this little chair with wheels. Emilio is about to show up. I sense his presence. Or maybe I just heard his van. Dale and I aren't finished here, but to Emilio that does not matter. Suddenly he's there in the doorway.

"Hey, you two, what's up?"

Dale looks up and breaks into a glorious smile. "Your dad's like going primal on me or some shit, and I don't know if I can take it."

"Hey, hey, that's not fair," I say.

"Yes, it is," says Dale.

Emilio steps into the studio. "Pops, I promised I would rescue her, okay? I'm taking her up to Rose Valley for a few hours." Emilio turns to Dale, "That good by you?"

"Yeah," says Dale. "I'd like that."

☙

BACA-

Dale leads the way down the pea gravel path. I pull Emilio aside and look into his eyes. "Don't lay too much metaphysical shit on her, okay?"

"Yeah?"

"Yeah. This girl, I think she's a witch."

Emilio laughs. Does this son of mine hear me? Of course not. He is 23 and a man. So he smiles at me, and just smiles and laughs and melts my heart and soul until I finally smile with him, trusting that all will be well.

DALE—

Emilio has this unbelievable charm. Not like forced, but true charm. I mean he's charming me, and he's charming Baca, and it's like you can't resist it. He's got us following him out to the driveway, and he's juggling two sets of keys in the air, like a real juggler you know, and he's riffing,

"Pops, you don't mind if we take the Volvo, do you? I'll trade you the van. Van for the Volvo, van for the Volvo."

"Uh…"

"Thanks." Emilio throws Baca his keys to the van, while he holds up the keys to the Volvo that he swiped off the shelf at the door.

Baca shouts out, "Hey, I don't want to be driving your van if…" But Emilio cuts him off.

"There's a fun-board in the back. You should run down to Mondo's."

Suddenly Baca freezes. I mean his face grows totally white and I'm staring at him like, Jesus, is this a stroke or something? Emilio acts like nothing happened, turning his back to sling his daypack into the backseat of the Volvo. Then he turns back to Baca and smiles at him, and that quick Baca comes back to life, the color rushing his cheeks. Emilio steps up to him and they kiss on the lips like a couple of Peruvians I guess…but to me it's so touching I need to take a deep breath. While Baca's standing there in some trance, Emilio's gesturing to me like, get in the car, quick, and I hop in and he backs out as Baca is looking at the keys in his hand, and then back at Emilio's parked van, and then he's shouting, "Hey, numb nuts, is there gas in this thing?!"

And Emilio smiles and shouts back, "That's up to you, Pops!"

And we're outta there.

⁂

DALE -

There's something really cool about being in a car with someone you really like, I mean really, and you're heading into the mountains and even though you think you're pretty cool, you have to recognize that he's very cool, and he's fucking handsome and I know he wants to get it on, right, so here we are, and I'm not even thinking about how it's gonna play out. Because it is what it is, okay? Whatever will be will be.

EMILIO—

I turn to this girl sitting alongside me. She's got me all happening right now. The way she handles herself. I smile at her and say, "Sometimes escaping from my Pops' orbit can be a fucking struggle. But that, that was pretty clean."

"That was deft."

"Whoa, deft, huh?"

"Yeah, deft. You're my hero. And where are you taking me?"

"To the moon." And now I know she's mine. I look over again. It's weird, how I've been with her, kissed her, but never really looked at her—it's been more her energy. So now I'm looking, and I see that she is truly beautiful. And it's almost like she does everything she can to deny it. Like fuck this, it's more of a burden than it's worth, but to me, to someone like me, that makes her even more beautiful. I soak her in.

DALE—

This guy is pretty trippy.

I'm looking out the windows and at first it's kinda dramatic, okay? We're heading into this steep canyon and the road's twisty and there's this creek down there and lots of rocks, and

89

we go through a couple of tunnels, and it's cool enough, but then we begin climbing, and I'm looking at these mountains and it's not like I pictured it I guess, like I was expecting some Swiss Alps thing or something, like Mother Theresa up there yodeling, I don't know. But these mountains, I mean they're big enough, but they're covered with all this scrub brush.

"Where are all the trees?"

"It's not like that. This whole Topa Topa range is chaparral. Semi-arid."

"Oh."

"The trees are along the creeks. Where the water is."

"Okay."

"That's where we're going."

Then we get quiet again and I'm feeling good with this guy, as the Volvo climbs up and up into the mountains, and then I turn and see the ocean. And I don't know what it is, the light, the reflection, I don't know but it gets me.

"Emilio, look, look!" and I realize it's the first time I'm saying his name, and he looks and says,

"Yeah," but then he goes real quiet. We turn a bend and the ocean is gone.

I wait a bit then ask him, "What are you thinking about?"

He doesn't answer. We climb up over the top of the ridge then he hangs a right onto a smaller road, "This is Rose Valley," he says.

"Yeah, okay, but what were you thinking about? What's with this ocean thing? What is that with you two? You and Baca?"

Emilio thinks about it. The Volvo's rolling down this smaller valley now, and it's feeling more remote.

"It was years ago…"

"Yeah?"

"You really wanna hear this?"

"Yeah."

RANIA—

I can just imagine what is going on up there in Ojai. I could cringe. But I won't. I am in my gallery selling an extremely expensive tapestry to an extremely wealthy businessman. My heart isn't in it, and I know I'm losing this sale. He isn't asking for much—some intelligent female energy, a touch of the cosmopolitan, a high-level flirtation with a hint of something more. All things I can deliver in my sleep. But not today. *Merde.* But I need the cash. I look this man in the eye.

"Mr. Fakhoury, may I be frank with you?"

"Of course, Rania."

"You know this, in the ways of business, there is always the need to keep current, and that from time to time, a business might fall short."

"Yes," he says. "Of course."

"So knowing my circumstance now, and me knowing how much you want this tapestry, I say to you, set your price and it is yours."

"Any price I want?"

"Any price you want." I'm hating myself. I hate this business. This cocksucker is about to teach his little Lebanese art dealer a lesson. Or maybe not. Maybe it worked. Finally he speaks up,

"My beautiful Rania. I respect your circumstances. I will pay full price for this tapestry under one condition. That for the next twelve months, anything for sale in your gallery, anything and everything, will be mine for half price."

"Up to three pieces," I counter.

"Five."

"Four."

"Four."

Goddamit. I love my fellow Arabs. I love them. I take his cash and live for another day.

⌘

BACA—

I feel fleeced by my own son. That's how you say it, no? Taken. By Emilio and it makes me smile. Because I know he is a good boy. Respectful. Raised right. And I wonder how all this will end up, remembering Rania's words, maybe this is heaven. Right here, right now.

⌘

EMILIO—

It is my most vivid memory. I almost never talk about it. But I know Dale asked me for a reason. I keep the Volvo on an even course as we roll into Rose Valley, and I tell her what happened.

"Okay, so I almost drowned. I was fourteen. There was this freaky winter northwest swell—it rolled down from Alaska and it caught Santa Cruz Island at just the right angle, okay? Just off the coast out there. And it bounced off the island and came charging across the channel, set after set. We got a call so we jumped in the van with our boards, my Pops driving me and my cousin G. He was like thirteen. Just this skinny little kid. Both of us. But he was a charger, right? Just like me.

"So we're driving down 33 and the wind was blowing and it's grey out, rain on the windshield, and I can tell my Pops was relieved pulling into C Street—'cause it's a mess there, the pier getting slammed and no one in the water. But me and my cousin G. we convince Pops to head up to State Beaches. Just to look at least, so we're on and off the 101 and Emma Woods is way too gnarly. I mean there are a few guys out there, but they're grown men, and they're gettin' fucking thrashed right, so there's no way. But G. and me, we got this bug now. We have to get in the water, so I tell the old man, what about Mondo's? See, it's a long shallow break. It's usually perfect for longboarders and grommets. It's gentle, it's a big cove and even on a day like today, it might be okay. So we drive up there and pull over and check it out.

BACA—

I didn't like it. I didn't like any of it. But also I knew, for a boy becoming a man, sometimes it must be his decision to enter the water.

EMILIO—

"So G. and me are outta the van and pulling on our wetsuits before Pops can say no, and it's freakin' wild out, you know, I mean the wind is blowing now, and these rollers are charging in and catching the break, and it's low tide 'cause otherwise like not a chance man, there'd be no beach, so we grab our boards and scramble down the rocks and I look back at Baca and he's reading things, and he starts shouting, "Get in at the point! Get up the beach! Up the beach!"

BACA—

So they do, you know. They run up the beach and I see Emilio getting ahead of G. and I'm thinking, shit, but I know they'll be okay right, because they're up the beach, and I see the current's gonna bring 'em right back at me, and maybe they'll catch a wave, or maybe not, but hey, they got in the water on the most gnarly day, and that's what they need.

EMILIO—

"We got as far as we could and leashed up and got in the water and it's friggen cold, and we gotta wade through some rocks and kelp, and it's raining now, I mean like stinging rain and the wind is blowing the tops off the waves, but they're still pounding in and I turn to G. and shout,

'Let's fucking do this, G.'

"And he's with me and finally we're in deep enough to jump on our boards and we're paddling across the break, figuring out what's what, and I look, and yeah, G.'s right there with me, and the next set comes rolling down on us and suddenly I'm like, oh fuck. Oh fuck."

BACA—

I made a mistake. The first wave caught them and broke and they went under, boards popping up, and then their heads, but the current had them, and that fast they were sweeping down the beach, unable to get in, or to get out, outside the waves. I saw G. throw a leg up over his board, Emilio just hanging on to his. I scrambled down the rocks, shouting and waving my arms for them to dig for the shore, to fight their way in but I could see the look in their eyes, like, hey, we're barely holding on out here. That fast they went past me. Down the beach, past the last stretch of sand, and after that only houses protected by a ragged wall of rocks. I ran for the van.

EMILIO—

"Okay, so it was fucked up right? But we got a handle on it, me and G. I finally rolled onto my board, and we were like whooshing down the beach, the waves bouncing off the rocks and comin' back at us almost as big as the ones crashing in on us from the ocean, but we both had our boards and we were together, duck-diving when we had to, shouting at each other. Stay together! Stay together! Then G. decided to make his move. I yelled at him, no. No!!!"

BACA—

I'm in the van, cranking down the highway. Looking through the cracks between the houses at the ocean, looking for these boys. Jesus, why did I let them in the water?

EMILIO—

"So how fucked up is this? G. makes his move at the wrong time and a wave smashes him into the rocks, and his board is gone, but I see him hanging onto the rocks, and his right arm is not working at all, and he's looking very disoriented. Very. And cold. Deep cold. But G.'s on the rocks now, and me, I'm still in the water and I'm thinking G. you stupid motherfucker—I was right—stay in the water—but I'm the one in trouble. I know it. I watch G. claw his way up the rocks, waves pounding him and his arm obviously all fucked up. He climbs up onto the highway and there are all these fucking idiots out there in slickers and boots and umbrellas and the fucking houses are starting to go, you know, cracking, like gun shots, and the boom of these waves and these shattering sounds and me clinging to my board, watching G. and hearing these people yelling at him, 'Hey, let us help you!' but instead he goes running up the highway yelling, "Uncle Baca! Uncle Baca!""

BACA—

Driving down in the van, I saw him running towards me, his right arm flopping. I stopped and he climbed in and he was shaking and in shock and I yelled at him, "Where's Emilio? Where is Emilio?" And finally G. says, he's still in the water. I drove on, yelling at him, tell me where, until finally he said, here, and there was a crowd of people and I jerked the van over and jumped out and looked down between the houses, the jumble of sharp rocks, the waves pounding, pounding, houses collapsing… And there he was. Emilio, clinging to his board, still caught in the break.

EMILIO—

"My muscles were breaking down. That's what happens. That's what I know now. In this situation, to this point of exhaustion, you just can't keep on, there isn't enough oxygen getting to the muscles to keep working. But what did I know? I was fourteen. I thought I knew enough to stay in the water until the right break in the waves. But then G. got out and here I am. I'm slipping off my board. I look up and see Pops climbing down the rocks. He's stripping down. Kicking off his shoes."

BACA—

He's lying. I froze. I froze on the rocks. I never jumped in and swam for him.

EMILIO—

"No, he did everything just right, 'cause just then a wave came, this weird gentle wave like the kind I started on like when I was three or something, and it swept me in and Baca was there, grabbing me, pulling me out, then covering me with his body as this huge pissed-off wave suddenly slammed down onto us. Then another. Then another. My Pops holding me onto the rocks until finally I caught my breath and we climbed the rocks to the highway."

❧

DALE—

"Wow." I'm sitting in the Volvo listening to this amazing story and all I can say is wow. Then Emilio says,

"Yeah. But you know what? After that? It was never the same between us. Between me and my Pops. Me and Baca."

We drive through this remote valley and then start climbing again, reaching another ridge and he pulls the car over and we get out and look down and across at a huge mass of white rocks. Huge. "Piedra Blanca," he says. "And straight below us, the Sespe River. It runs west to east, over thirty miles, without a dam or house or anything. And at the hot springs, it turns south, down through the gorge and out at Fillmore where it joins the Santa Clara River."

"Hah," I say. Men and their maps. Men and their maps and the maps in their minds.

He drives the Volvo down this twisty road, and we pull into a dirt lot under some pine trees and he's talking on and on about how this all got changed a few years ago because some environmental group sued the forest service to protect some toad and they actually won the case, so they tore out Lion Campground and that's okay actually because it got to be mostly bikers and cholos, back in the day, and the vibe became very uncool, and I'm sitting here listening, in this daze now, this total love daze. I don't know what else to call it. His words. The way he smells. The idea of touching him again. Kissing him.

We get out of the car. It's quiet here. Warm and quiet, a little breeze through the pines and everything smells really good. He pulls his daypack out and lays it on the hood. "Did you sunscreen?"

"What? No."

"Come here, I'll sunscreen you."

So I walk around the car and I feel totally comfortable standing in front of him and putting out my arms, presenting my bare skin to him. He takes sunscreen from his pack and squeezes some into his palms, and he's all sensible, spreading it over my arms, my hands, and when he tells me to spread my legs a bit I do and he squats in front of me and rubs the sunscreen over my thighs, my knees, my calves. Then he stands up and looks at me and smiles, "You are the whitest girl I've ever known."

"Yeah, well, I'm a city rat."

"No, you're not. You got no tats. You're a nature girl. Close your eyes."

So I do and I feel him sunscreening my nose, my cheeks and forehead, my throat, the back of my neck, and then suddenly his lips are on mine. He's kissing me, and I open my mouth to his and today he tastes like coffee and Altoids and I am the happiest girl in the world. Here it is. Here it is.

❧

EMILIO—

As I lead her down to the river I'm saying to myself, are you really doing this? 'Cause maybe my Pops is right, maybe… So I decide not to decide, to get her down as far as Bear Creek, then see where it's at. I take lead on the narrow trail down to the river. We flatten out and clear some bulrushes and Dale gets her first real view of the Sespe. The water's up, almost waist-deep and flowing steady across a broad bed of river rocks. Someone's built a place to rock-hop it, but it looks pretty sketchy.

We take our shoes and socks off, and tie them together and dangle them around our necks, and holding hands we step into the water and she gasps, because this is no pond, I mean this shit is moving, and the water up here is chilly and the rocks under our feet are round and full of surprises. She squeezes my hand. But she's game, and we make it across.

We plop down in the sun to dry our feet. As we pull our socks on, I look up at her, and I feel a rush of love for this girl.

Love.

I take a deep breath. Then I lead her on, down the Sespe River trail, leading us both down into a wild place.

❧

DALE—

We're holding hands because this part of the trail is wide enough actually being a fire road at one time as Mr. Factoid just told me. And we're walking on and on and it's hot and dusty and I'm not really seeing too much of the river, like it's down there to the right where I can see trees, but up here on the trail it's hot, and so again it's not like I thought it was gonna be but who's complaining because every ten minutes or so we stop, and Emilio kisses me and smiles and laughs, and pulls the steel water bottle out of his pack, and we drink and walk on. And then, right out of the blue, Emilio says, "So what's the deal with you?"

"What?"

"You know. Everybody's got some kinda deal. I told you something about me. What about you?"

"What did you tell me? You fell in the ocean. Your old man was there. You got out."

"Hey."

"Sorry. All right. I'm not trying to make it trivial. It's just, you know… this kinda trauma stuff, it can be stuff like that, or a car crash or something, or then it can get deeper, you know. Into a dark place. And I don't want to go there."

"Like a sexual place."

"Yeah. Maybe. Yeah. And I don't want to go there."

"Okay. Hey, okay."

I see him caring about me. We walk on. I ask him, "What about you, Mr. Natural? What's your deep sexual secret?"

"You really want to know?"

"I really wanna know."

99

"Okay, so my Swedish hippie mother breastfed me until way past when. Til I could ask for tittie in three different languages. So top that, Dale. Dale of Green Acres."

And I just have to laugh until he pulls me tight and envelopes my body with his—his hard chest and flat belly pressed up against me, strong arms around me, his hips brushing into mine. We're a good fit, Emilio and me. And I can smell him, the sweat and sunscreen, his pores open and his body sending out all sorts of chemicals that have my body tingling and surging with this energy that I've never really felt before. It's like it's sexual, but it's not in my pussy, it's deeper somehow, at the very bottom of my spine, near my ass, and I'm remembering what someone was talking about—kundalini—maybe the guy up at the meditation place, maybe Baca even, about this creative, loving lust energy thing and I'm telling myself, shut up. Just shut the fuck up and feel it. So I do.

❧

RANIA—

This Blue Monday afternoon I take Mr. Fakhoury's cash to the bank and then I'm on my own. I know they are together, Dale and Emilio. I can feel their tenderness and love. I want so hard to be happy for them, but it's not in me. All the love, understanding, maturity I believe I've achieved, it is now out the window. I am distraught, and that is not like me.

❧

BACA—

Me neither. I'm about to head down to Ventura, brown-bag a quart of Sierra Nevada and grab some fish and chips on the pier. Maybe catch the sunset. Or maybe an early fog. I'll bring my poncho. Fit right in with the other low-lifes.

EMILIO—

We're maybe a mile from Bear Creek crossing, and I'm glad that Dale's keeping up. I mean she's strong, this girl. She's fit, and I'm thinking okay, maybe she'll be down with this plan, maybe I'll just lay it on her, but then suddenly I stop and pull her to a stop too. There's a snake on the trail, asleep in the sun.

"What?" she says.

"Rattlesnake. See it?"

"Oh, Jesus."

"It's okay," I say. "It's crashed out, couldn't move if it wanted to. We'll just step around it."

"No way."

"No, it's easy. Watch."

And I step over the snake and I see it open one eye, but this snake is harmless, I know it, so it's fun for me now to look back to Dale and smile and say, "You gotta trust me on this one."

Dale's staring at me, her mind buzzing. "No way," she says. "I'm not doing this. Throw a rock at it or something. Get it outta here."

"I'm not throwing a rock at it. You have to trust me."

She says, "Okay, so maybe this stupid snake isn't gonna bite me. So I step over it and it doesn't bite me just like you said. Then what? You fucking own me?"

"Huh, what?" She can get into some very weird thinking, this girl. Suddenly I'm impatient and I'm like, "Listen, we got a ways to go here, and I'm goin' on, and you can follow me, or I'll catch you on the way back. Your choice."

DALE—

So much for the lovey-dovey. Jesus. I watch Emilio head off down the trail. And suddenly I'm stepping around this snake and that quick its head comes up, and the rattle goes haywire and I'm like fucking peeing my shorts running to Emilio, throwing myself into his arms screaming, "Fuck! Fuck! Fuck!" And he's all laughing, and finally I calm down as he says look, look back, and so I look back and sure enough, the snake's just lying there, dead to the world, and I look to Emilio—like, did you do that? I stare into his eyes, and he just smiles and part of me, this little slice of me deep inside, says, okay, you're gonna play it that way…

And then I do the obvious thing. To throw him off. I walk past him and set a faster pace, and it's feeling good, I'm feeling the power and love and sex of it, and suddenly the trail curls around a high bend and we're overlooking this amazing vista—I see the river, cool and silver, running through the rocks, and the trees tall on the opposite bank, and beyond that, I don't know, but I see how the trail is getting us to a place I want to go be so I keep walking fast, with Emilio behind me yelling, "Hey, Amelia Earhart, what's the rush?"

And I'm yelling back at him, "Hey, asshole, I know who Amelia Earhart is, okay? I fucking know."

And now we're both laughing again knowing that I don't have a clue, and he doesn't either, not really, and now he runs up behind me, and it's hot and sweaty and dusty and I'm feeling kinda spent, but he grabs me from behind and wraps me up as I bend over, and it's kinda dumb but we're doin' this little quiet circling love thing right there in the trail when some guy walks around the bend, carrying a fishing pole and wearing chest waders and he really just looks so stupid that Emilio and I start laughing as the guy comes flopping past and Emilio asks him, all innocent like, "Catch anything?"

And the guy's so bent out of joint he yells back, "Yeah, my dick!" and we laugh some more.

EMILIO—

A half mile further, I cut off down a short twisting trail to the river, pulling Dale along. "We call this place Henry Moore."

It's where the Sespe narrows and carves through a series of big red boulders, all round and smooth, all these great shapes, one after another, the river flowing through them, creating eddies, pools, small waterfalls, rock slides. I guide Dale down onto the flattest rock and we sit.

The sun is hot, the rock is hot. I see her crab down and squat at the water's edge, cupping her hands.

"Don't," I say.

"Why not?"

"Giardia. It's a microbe in the water. Livestock. We gotta filter it. Here, drink this." I toss her the steel water bottle.

"We can swim though, right?"

"Yeah, we can swim."

And just like that she strips off her shoes and socks, pulls off her shirt and stands up and pulls down her shorts and underwear, never once looking at me, as if I wasn't even there, and she steps into the water, then does a shallow dive into the small pool. I see her under the water, her crazy dark hair now streaming short and sleek, her arms reaching, her white ass spreading as her legs frog-kick her across the pool with one smooth kick. She comes up on the other side and finds the bottom with her feet and stands up, half in, half out, leaning against a slab of rock. She turns my way, then tilts her head back, catching the sun on her face, and her breasts are small and high, nipples taut, and her belly is white and round. I'm looking at this beautiful woman, this long body filled with surprises, this deep soul, and I truly don't know what to think. Only what I see. Only what I feel.

She shouts to me, "Are you coming in?"

I feel the erection in my shorts. "No. This pool isn't big enough for the two of us."

"What then?"

"Let me ask you something."

"What?"

"Will you spend the night with me?"

"Yeah. Yes."

"Out here I mean. In the woods."

"Uh, sure. Doesn't it get cold?"

"Yeah, it gets cold. And there'll be some dew."

I stare at her staring back at me, and there's something in this girl's eyes, it's like okay—any challenge, anything, and she's there.

"Okay," she says.

"Good. But we gotta book. It's another three miles."

❦

BACA—

It is difficult to be an adult. In these times? And to be a parent? Some days I just want to curl up on the couch, yes? And be quiet. Even when I am in control of my personal life, the big picture is all too much. And it is at these moments that I better understand my Ojai friends' quests for deeper spirituality. My view is a bleak view, I know, but when you see how futile this crazy planet is, so maybe you find it easier to get through each day knowing you're halfway onto the next thing anyway.

Ha. Bah. Bah humbug. I laugh at myself in my poncho. This is the state of mind that a quart of Sierra Nevada and some greasy fish and chips will buy you on a foggy day on the pier in Ventura.

RANIA—

I'm not drinking beer on the Ventura pier. I'm grinding away on a treadmill upstairs at the Santa Monica Y, surrounded by like-minded souls. Below us, we can see through the glass down below, the lap pool, and at this time in the afternoon suddenly the pool deck floods with children in bathing suits, adjusting their caps, shivering and fidgeting and feeling the incredible prepubescent tension of boys and girls together, waiting for their coach to bark them into the water. And then there's the coach, and that's what she does, and that's what I watch as I monitor my heartbeat at a steady 125 to 130 and I feel the pores open and the sweat break out evenly and I ask God to take care of them. The children. Take care of the children.

℥

DALE—

So now that's it's decided and I'm back in my clothes, I guess I'm supposed to just go into squaw mode or something, the way Emilio is striding out ahead of me. But I'm in, right? I'm in. So a ways past Henry Moore we hit these sandy beaches at Bear Creek crossing, and now we got some serious trees happening, I don't know what they are, but they're beautiful and it's shady and I'm thinking can't we just stay here? But instead he just keeps plowing on, me matching his stride. And then we have to cross the river again and do the whole shoe thing, and I'm feeling a little cranky now so I say screw it so I'll get my shoes wet, BFD, and he laughs and decides to do the same, so we wade through the Sespe, and it's not like we're carrying packs or anything, except for his day pack, so the current's easy enough, and then we're up on some narrow trail that starts cutting across this steep mountainside and I'm yelling at him, hey what happened to the fire road and he's yelling back, washed out. Way back when.

తు

EMILIO—

I'm taking her to Sandy Bend.

When the trail crosses the water again we abandon it and stay with the river. Boulder-hopping, but now that our shoes are wet, it's easier and the river gets broad and shallow through here. But I can see she's feeling beat, so we stop in the shade of a cottonwood, our feet in ankle deep water, leaning against a rock. I pull a couple of bananas and an oatmeal bar from my pack and we eat them. I tuck the tin foil wrapper back into the pack, but toss the banana peels under a bush. "Ssshh. Don't tell anyone."

"Oh, who am I gonna tell, Manny?"

"What?"

"Nothing."

A quarter mile further we're at Sandy Bend.

తు

DALE—

It's perfect. The perfect place. The river riffing through the rocks, and you can hear it rushing, you know, the water sound, as the river gets narrow and then all comes together and hangs a left and sweeps into this deep pool. There's this sandy beach on one side, our side, and straight across this very large rock, the kind you can dive off, and I'm thinking please, God, please tell me this is where we're gonna spend the night. And I look up at Emilio and say,

"Tell me this is where we're gonna spend the night."

"This is where we're gonna spend the night."

I plop down in the sand and take off my wet shoes and socks. It's still hot, but I know this won't last forever. I turn to Emilio.

"So, Tarzan, whaddaya got in mind here?"

He laughs.

"I mean are you gonna build us a cabin or something?"

He shakes his head no.

"But there's no way we can walk out tonight."

He laughs. "No. We're in."

I lie back down onto the warm sand and spread my arms and legs to the sun. Fuck it. We're in.

EMILIO—

I've got these friends, these older guys from Ventura Search and Rescue, plus a couple of us younger guys, and we all talked about the same thing, how great it would be to walk in and you knew you'd have what you needed, already there. I mean bags, pads, tent… So we made it happen. It's simple, a steel locker. And you hide it in the most gnarly place you can find, and then it's there for you. So I walk away from Dale and back into the chaparral—thorny, prickly shit but I go into my nature mode and slip through and it's there, half-buried, covered with some mesquite branches. I push them aside, undo the clasp and swing the lid open. It's all there, plus a mess kit and grill, toilet paper, some canned food, coffee and a couple of bottles of expensive red wine with this message taped to them—"If you drink one of these, you'd better replace it by the time I return. Bill (Mad Dog) Slaughter." I laugh and start hauling out the gear and provisions.

DALE—

I'm lying in the sand, the heat of the sun, the gurgling water, and Emilio coming and going, shuffling around in the afternoon heat. And finally I'm getting the beauty of this place. It's harsh. The mountains are hard and sharp and covered with bristle. It's not all Bambi and Thumper. But along the river, like here at Sandy Bend, in a spot like this… It's as if the harshness makes these little places so special. Little pockets in the wilderness where you can find shelter. The sun beats down on my eyelids. I'm trying to remember who I am, where I am. I hear his voice,

"You like the stars, right?"

"Yeah."

"So we're not gonna need a tent."

"Okay."

"Don't mind a little dew?"

"I'm not sure what that means." I still have my eyes closed. Half the fucking conversations I have with this guy feel like I'm in a dream. Or underwater. But it's warm. And it's okay. And I actually fall asleep for a bit.

EMILIO—

As Dale sleeps I set up camp. There's a water filter pump and a big glass jug, so I spend the time to pump us a gallon of drinkable water from the river. Then I head downstream and gather some deadwood from a cottonwood grove. Enough to keep a small fire burning late. I'm happy. I'm hot and sweating, feeling in touch with the Chumash who did the exact same thing right here, centuries ago. Back at camp Dale's asleep and I strip naked out of my shorts and shirt and wade into the pool. It's deep and cool and I slip underwater and stay there, looking for a rare steelhead, but there are only small trout and some crappies. When I surface, she's sitting up, staring at me. "Hi," I say.

"Hi," she answers. "I fell asleep."

"Come on in."

"Maybe later."

"Suit yourself."

DALE—

I watch as he swims and dives under and he swims like a seal, all smooth and sleek and fluid. And then he surfaces and stands and wades out of the water. Coming right towards me, his hair slicked back, revealing his shoulders, his chest with a patch of golden brown hair, and his strong arms, then his flat stomach, rippled with muscles, and his hair is dripping and his skin is bronze, no tan lines, not for this nature boy, and he's got this grin on his face walking out, revealing himself, his dick and balls tight with the cold, then his strong thighs, and I don't know what to do, what to say, so I take a deep breath and say, "Whoooo..." and I lie back down on the sand and close my eyes as he lies down on his back, right alongside me, his wet skin on the hot sand. He closes his eyes and we're quiet.

Then I feel something happening, how he's sliding his breathing into mine, until we're both in sync, lying there, flush to the hot sun, him naked. And me just knowing he's naked alongside me, I can't help myself, I turn my head and open my eyes and I see his chest gently rising and falling with each breath and I glance down and see that his penis has relaxed and fleshed out and I feel this surge of lust overcome me, and I fight the urge to bend over and take him in my mouth, just like that, suck him in between my lips, and wrap my tongue around him and make him wet with my spit and feel him grow inside my mouth, and I feel my twat go all hot and liquid and my breasts are swelling and I try to control myself, chill it, but he's gotta be feeling all this energy I'm putting out because suddenly his cock begins to grow, all on its own, lengthening, growing fuller with blood, and needing to swing up and free itself from between his thighs, and it's the most amazing thing, without a word, without a single touch or moan or anything, his eyes still closed as his beautiful cock grows and creeps over his right thigh and hip bone, growing thicker and longer, until finally it's lifting off the flat of his flank and sliding across his belly until it's past his navel, rising in the air now at an angle, rigid in the air, where it moves with his breathing and I'm thinking this is not an invitation, this is just some trippy guy I like who's really in touch somehow, I don't know, so I lie my head back down and catch my breath and finally tell him, "I'm sorry, but you gotta put that thing away."

"Sorry." And he rolls over onto his chest. "But that's you making that happen. That's not me."

I turn my head and he's gazing at me, his blue eyes so intense, his back and ass and legs covered with the hot white sand and suddenly I'm tearing my clothes off and running and jumping into the river, the clear deep water, going under, chilling my fire, but then even underwater I hear his splash and there he is, his hair all seaweed, grinning at me, grabbing me, spinning me around, pressing his body against mine. We surface and kiss and hold each other. And I kiss him again and laugh and say, "That wasn't fair."

"What?"

"You know what. That. On the beach."

And he laughs and splashes me, then swims away.

❦

DALE—

And so we spend the afternoon like that, swimming, rolling in the hot sand, kissing. Not in a rush now. Now that we know what the night has to offer.

It's hot, and the sun is still strong. Emilio keeps trying to cover me, with clothes, with sunscreen, but I'm loving it, the sun. Loving it on my white skin until finally he drags me to this big sprawling tree with these floppy green, yellow, brown leaves. "It's a sycamore," he says.

It's got these big fat branches, low to the ground, and they're going every which way, and one of them, it just draws me to it. I walk over and rub my hand along it. You can bend over it, it's that low, and big around as a horse almost, you could roll right onto it, and the bark is smooth like it knows what's it's meant for, smooth because so many couples before us used this branch and wore the skin right off it. And so I stand next to it and rub my hand along it, but Emilio says,

"No. Let's just sit in the shade."

"Hey, lover boy. I was imagining…"

"I know. Don't. That branch, it has bad energy."

"What?"

"Things happened on that branch that shouldn't have."

"Tell me."

"Bad things. Everyone knows this. My friend Julie, she's Chumash, right? When she sat under this tree, it was very clear to her. Now leave it alone."

So he pulls me to the far side of the tree, under higher branches, and we sit in the sand in the shade and he hugs me and kisses me and he gets all serious.

"You're attracted to the dark side."

"I guess. I don't want to be."

"If you ever want to talk to me, about what happened to you, you can. I can hear it."

"Thanks." And I can feel his warmth and care and love, the way he's staring into my eyes and smiling. Loving me. Loving me through all my hurt and anger and fucked up past.

"Let me show you a trick you can use, for when the pain is too much."

"Okay," I say.

"I want you to remember your best moment in life. Your very best moment."

"Like what?"

"Anything. Like for me, the moment I use is from when I was five and on a beach with Baca and my Mom, and I was between them holding their hands and they were swinging me back and forth. Something like that."

"I don't have something like that. From when I was a kid, no way."

"Okay, so later, then. Think."

So I think about it, and slowly a smile comes to my face, and I'm remembering, and I say—"When I was fourteen, when I ran away from Ohio. I had it all planned out, I saved my money, I already bought the bus ticket and I forged this very convincing letter from my father that I was visiting my uncle in Van Nuys. I had my bag packed and my friend Liz drove me to the station, and then me getting on, with my skinny legs and black leather jacket and that bus driving off, that was the best feeling of my life."

"Good. So here's the exercise. Find a place on your body that you can touch, non-sexual, so maybe your forehead, your neck, maybe your other hand. Find a place that feels natural."

I think, then with my right hand I pinch the base of my left thumb, that fleshy part, and it feels good to me. "Okay, I got it."

"Good. So feel that touch, and remember that day back in Ohio when you finally broke free. When you recognized your love for yourself, your worth, and you broke free to start a new life. And how good that felt."

"Yeah."

"Okay, that's it."

"That's it?"

"Yeah. From now on, whenever you need reinforcement, about who you really are, just touch yourself like that and you'll have it. It's called anchoring a magical state."

"You sound like your old man."

"Nah. It's all Rania. And my mom."

℘

BACA—

This kind of stuff, I don't mind him going there with her. It's harmless. It's helpful. It's like her symbol this morning. These are tools, you see. Ways of smoothing the path, reclaiming balance.

℘

RANIA—

I have a stone that I carry with me everywhere. Whenever I feel afraid or lost I hold it in my hand and it comforts me. I'm holding it now.

℘

EMILIO—

The afternoon is sliding. There's a stand of tall firs at the bend of the river and now their shadows lengthen along the sand as the sun settles into evening. I look over at Dale. She's got her t-shirt and shorts on, walking back from the tree to our little stretch of beach. I'm suddenly starving and I shout out, "Hey, are you hungry?" And she yells back,

"Starving."

I run up to her and wrap my arms around her. I smell her, I take her in with each hug, each touch. "Okay, you got two choices, chili with meat or chili with no meat."

"No meat."

"Liar."

"I'm serious. I got you."

I have her dig a shallow fire pit as I open the mess kit and pull out an army knife then slice open the twenty-four ounce can of vegetarian chili. Dale piles up way too much of the firewood I gathered, so we pick some out and slip some dry grass tinder underneath it, and I hit the lighter and that fast we have fire. She's beautiful in the firelight with the sun setting behind us and the quiet crackle of the fire and ripple of the river, and if you're listening, the sounds of frogs and crickets, poking around, making noise, looking for love.

Dale looks at me. "Now what? How do we cook this stuff?"

I say, watch, and I add some more wood to the fire, then lift the open can of chili and place it right into the flames. She laughs. I look at her. "Want some wine?"

"Oh, yeah."

So I grab a bottle of red and open it and pour half the bottle into a big metal mug and we each take a sip, and it's very good, smooth and round. We're sitting on our pads now, in front of the little fire, shoulder to shoulder, drinking red wine, kissing, watching our chili boil over until I finally wrestle the can out of the coals and Dale finds two spoons and we eat.

The sky grows dark and the stars arrive overhead.

❧

DALE—

On this little stretch of sand along the Sespe. The sun is gone and it's hard to see. Emilio and me start arranging the pads, opening up the sleeping bags, him pointing out where our heads should be 'cause of the slight rise of the beach. And I say, so where do I pee? And he says, anywhere, so I wander down the beach a bit and drop my shorts and squat and think jeez, am I gonna fuck this guy tonight, and I tell myself no, no, we're gonna make love.

When I'm back at the fire, Emilio's walking in a circle around our bags dropping small stones in the sand.

"What's this about?"

"Nothing. Just a habit. When I'm out in the woods like this."

"This is some voodoo thing, isn't it?"

"Yeah. Voodoo love."

So we step together into this circle of stones and we stand there on our sleeping bags and we slowly undress each other, then we sink down to the bags and it's kind of a mess of zippers and folds 'cause they're mummy bags and they don't lie flat, but somehow he eases me onto an open bag and he runs his fingers across my neck, down to my breast where he draws a circle around my small round boob, and my nipple aches for his touch, but he moves on, just going slow, so slow. Then I kiss him and I can feel him doing that slow breath thing again, trying to slow me down, get me in rhythm, but I'm feeling this sexual urgency now and I run my hand across his flat belly and then I wrap my fingers around his erection and it's one thing to see it, you know, but now, to have it in my hand. To feel the heft and swell of it. I hear him groan and I go straight down on him and that fast I have him in my mouth and my whole body shudders with this rush of masculine energy that I'm receiving through my mouth, deep in my mouth, down my throat and throughout my body.

EMILIO—

I'm losing her. She's losing me. I jerk away. I lost her, whoever she is. That fast—it doesn't feel right to me. She looks up and says, "What? What!?"

I answer, "Hey…"

I roll away onto my back but my hard-on isn't going anywhere and she rolls on top of me and slides her breasts over my dick and up my chest until she's kissing me again, and I'm there with her and I'm not. I'm there with her and I'm not.

"Just fuck me," she says. "Right now, just like this. I want you to fuck me, to have you inside me. I'll straddle you. I'm so wet you won't know what hit you. I'm so hot I'll burn you up. I will, I'll burn you up."

I stare into her eyes and I feel her overpowering me, her sex so strong, as she slaps my chest with her hands, her voice full of force,

"I want you. Don't you get this? I want you."

"I get it. But we're not in sync. We're rushing it here."

"Yeah. That's how I want it. Just like that!"

And now she's got my dick in her hands and I swear her eyes are almost rolling back in her head as she rides me and I'm like, uh oh, oh man, oh fuck, and she's spreading her legs and lowering herself down onto me and suddenly this voice tells me, no way you're puttin' your dick inside this girl tonight. No way. So I grab her hands and she fights me. Wordless. Both of us. Not a word, straining, arms strong against arms, staring at each other, and she tries to squirm her pussy down onto my dick and I roll her off and roll on top of her and I hold her hands down, sprawled across the bags and sand and I can feel the damp and grit of it against us, and when she spreads her legs I spread mine further, out over hers and slowly vise them together.

I whisper, "Enough. Enough."

"Hit me," she whispers. "Hit me with your hand. Hit me with your belt."

"Dale…"

"Take me out of this fucking circle. Bend me over that tree and do me."

And now she's crying and I'm trying to wipe her tears and kiss her cheeks saying, hey, hey, it's okay, when suddenly she's like,

"Fuck you, Emilio! Fuck you!" and she jumps up and grabs a sleeping bag and strides off down the beach. I watch her move away. Her sunburnt ass is the last thing I see disappear from the firelight into the dark.

Shit. Now what? I throw another stick on the fire. It's gonna be a long night.

DALE—

I'm down the beach. I throw the sleeping bag down on the sand. I walk to the water's edge. Then I turn and find myself drawing a circle in the sand. Then I put a slash through it. I don't know what I'm doing. Something Baca taught me.

EMILIO—

I give her about thirty minutes then I grab the small flashlight and find her down the beach, sitting up in her bag, all quiet. I squat down beside her.

"Listen," I say. "Come back to the fire. To the circle. Come back. We don't need to say another word. It's chilly out. We'll climb into our bags and I'll spoon you, okay? And we'll get our energy flowing the right way again, just by snuggling up like that, okay? Say okay."

"Okay…"

So we walk back up the beach to the fading fire. We're both still naked, Dale dragging her mummy bag behind her. We step into the circle. I straighten our pads out, then brush the sand off my feet, climb into my bag and zip it up. She does the same. She rolls onto her side and I snuggle up against her and we spoon. There's a long silence, but I know she wants to talk.

"You get off on that, right? Rough and fast."

"Yeah, sometimes. I don't know. I don't know how to get rid of it."

"Yeah."

"I love you, Emilio. I love you, and I want to express that, but I've got all this shit going on inside me."

"So let it out."

"Yeah."

"But there's better ways of doing it."

"What'd you mean?"

"We can explore anyplace we want. You can work things out through stories. That's what the ancients did. You don't have to act out. But you've got to do it in a safer container."

"I feel safe here."

"Safe enough to visit the dark side?"

There's a long silence as she considers.

"Only if you're willing," I add.

"I'm willing."

☙

RANIA—

This is where I am uncomfortable.

BACA—

Me too. Although I am a great believer in fantasy. It's safe because in personal fantasy, you are the creator, all of it is an output of your own mind, your own soul.

RANIA—

But that's not this. Here it's Emilio imposing his story onto Dale.

BACA—

I don't know that? That is my point. He thinks he knows what she needs.

RANIA—

Emilio is too young.

BACA—

So all I can say to him is, Son, do as I do, not as I don't do. Or something like that.

RANIA—

Baca, I told you to keep a tight leash on him.

BACA—

As if I have any control.

℃

EMILIO—

We lie there, each naked, cocooned in our own bags, spooning, connected by energy but separated by layers of zippers and smooth nylon and goose down. I don't say anything for the longest time. She senses my worry. But I know she wants to hear this story. That she's ready to go there with me. But this is on her now, to let me know. And then I hear her whisper,

"Tell me what happened. On the branch. Tell me."

"I don't know what happened."

"You know. You know."

I think for a moment, then begin,

"This happened long ago. It's not you, right? This is not you."

"I know."

I slip into a semi-whisper, wanting to mesmerize her, but that's stupid because she is so suggestible already, so willing to go anywhere you take her.

"There was a girl," I say, "A young woman of a tribe who lived along this river, and she was the most desirable of all the girls. And she knew it, and she turned mean about it because she knew her fate was not to have a husband, not to live a full life, but instead to be sacrificed to a creature in the forest. A creature half man, half animal who was a great threat to the tribe. Each year at the summer solstice, the tribe brought their

119

most beautiful daughter down to the river, and here they strip her naked and bend her over a low tree branch, a branch just like our sycamore."

"Yes."

"And with leather strips they tie her right hand to her right ankle, and her left hand to her left ankle, and they leave her there like that all day, her stomach pressed against the smooth round tree branch, her ass in the air, her breasts hanging free, her wrists and ankles burning with the bite of the rawhide."

"Yes."

"She knows not to call out. She knows her fate. The shadows lengthen and the sun sets. But on this night, there are no crickets or frogs. There is not even the sound of the river. There is only silence."

I glance at the small fire, dwindling to coals. I decide it's safe enough to go on.

"The day's heat grows cool in the night. Then suddenly there is a charge that runs through her. She can feel him coming up behind her. Soundless. The girl's skin flushes with goose bumps. The fine hairs on your arms, on the back of your neck, on the small of your back—they rise and stiffen. You feel a shiver between your thighs."

"Yes."

"You smell me before you feel me. I smell of man and animal. There's a deep bite to my scent that activates all your senses. Your wrists hurt. You feel the helplessness of your position. But part of you welcomes this. You want it like this. Total surrender. You want me to take you."

"Yes."

"You're cold but hot, your stomach pressed up against the smooth bark of the sycamore, your nipples erect, but still your thighs squeezed tight. You hear my breath and in that sound you hear the deepest longing. My deepest desire. For you. To have you. I want you. And I will have you."

"Yes."

"Now, you feel it between your legs, a jolt of energy, electricity, opening your blood vessels. The blood engorging your sex, your lips, your clit and deep in your vagina, you feel that, yes? As you grow wet for me."

"Yes. Yes."

"You feel my hot breath on your neck. The full length of my body pressing up against you, and you're startled by me down below. You feel coarse fur, sharp knees pressing into your thighs, and a phallus like none you've ever imagined. But I am pure man up above, draped over your back, my bare chest, my powerful arms, my lips and hot breath on your neck. Suddenly I pull back off you. To look you over, your long white body draped over the branch, your arms and legs extended downwards, lashed together, your face hidden, your white ass arched in the air and you can feel me behind you, how much I want you. To have you. To fuck you."

"Yes."

"So you spread your legs, your fingers and toes barely reaching the sand, rustling the leaves and now you're aware of every sound, every sensation—the frogs, the crickets, the river, the dew beginning to form, the cool breeze wafting up between your thighs as your pussy burns with heat, your entire body pulsing with sex. You're opening yourself up, preparing yourself. Offering yourself. You feel all my masculine power massing behind you. All the strength and vitality and lust building beyond my control. The phallus growing longer and harder than before, throbbing between the white round cheeks of your ass. Wanting you. You. To shove apart your thighs and own you.

"Instead, I grasp your hair. Pull your face up, into the night air. My lips on your neck, your cheek. You begin to cry out and suddenly my hand is over your mouth and two fingers part your lips and you suck on them and you feel how it's all connected—from ass to fingers to mouth to tongue to cock to cunt. You suck on my fingers then wet them with your spit because you know my intentions don't you? Don't you?"

"Yes."

"I pull my wet fingers from your mouth and you arch your back, ass rising in the night air and I run my hand between your thighs finding your beautiful pussy and you are dripping so wet and hot there is no need for saliva as my fingers spread open your beautiful petals, your labia, opening you and suddenly the scent of your cunt hits my nostrils and fills me with lust and I growl and bite into your neck."

"Yes."

"I push against you, my phallus groping for your hole. We're both panting, sweating..."

And here I stop for a moment to catch my breath, my own erection about to burst with cum right in the sleeping bag. Dale, zipped into her bag, spoons deeper into my pelvis, and her whisper is suddenly throaty, threatening, "Tell me. Tell me what happens."

I feel the energy shifting in her voice, something is different.

"Tell me," she growls.

I go on, "The tip of my phallus finds the wet of you and you try to twist away and I snarl. You strain against your bonds—the rawhide wet now with your sweat, cutting into your wrists and ankles. Suddenly you want to feel your own power, to touch me. To dig your nails into my back, my ass. To grab my cock with both hands, to take me in your mouth and suck, then drop onto your back and spread your..."

"No, No, I want to just fuck you. Fuck you just the way you are. Bent over the tree. I want to take my dick and ram it into you."

"Whoa, whoa..." I say, realizing that she's reversing roles, "Don't go there."

"What?!" she suddenly yells. "Fuck you then!"

Dale rolls away in her sleeping bag, then spins around to face me, eyes glaring in the firelight. "It's what I want, it's what I deserve!"

"Hey, it's okay," I say. "Easy." And I'm thinking wow, this girl's tripping on me, but it kind of pisses me off and makes me scoff and I say, "Whose story is this anyway?"

She's quiet. Then she gets a grip and laughs, squirming in her bag and she makes a face at me. "So I stole your story, so what?"

I roll and think about it. Staring up into the sky. And first I think selfishly, think how glad I am that I didn't fuck her. But then I just grow deflated. Tired. Feeling lost and without the energy to find the light.

And that's how we end the night. Filled with frustrated sexual energy. Uncertain love. And disconnect.

I sit up and pour the last of the wine into the metal mug. "Want some?"

"No."

So I gulp it and lie back down on the sand alongside her. I see that she has unzipped her bag a bit, letting in some breeze to cool her body. We stare up at the stars, the Milky Way. I reach and take her hand.

"Thanks for bringing me," she says.

"You're welcome." And as we drift off to sleep, I wonder, is she welcome? Or am I gonna get burned here…

❧

BACA—

We're all getting burned, that's the point.

RANIA—

Why do we do this to ourselves?

BACA—

Because it's more interesting than watching the Lakers?

DALE—

I gotta say, waking up this morning, I'm gonna sleep in a mummy bag from now on. Maybe this is all I need. Stay wrapped up in a goose down cocoon, hands to myself. I think and wonder about how crazy I was last night. To him. Emilio. I figure he'll let me know, one way or another.

Emilio's got a fire going, a black pot of boiling water sitting in the coals. I realize it's chilly and I snuggle deeper into the bag. Staring at him. This man.

He's rigging some system to make coffee and he's got this big smile on his face and the smoke from the fire drifts over me and I am awash in this man. I am in love with him.

"Hey, what's up?" I say.

"Coffee. You slept."

"Oh, yeah."

"Dreams?"

"Are you kiddin' me? My brain was like, okay, leave me the fuck alone. After last night, *no mas!*"

He laughs and I know now that when I'm with him I can say anything, be anything, and I don't have to suddenly feel that I'm out there on a limb, that I'm sayin' something stupid, or he's looking at me funny. I know that he's there for me. He's there. I love him and he loves me back.

But then he changes the energy.

I stare into his milky blue eyes and ask, "What?"

"Yeah, well, you know I'm young and this may sound stupid, but I've been thinking about this. About how it went last night. And I want you to know that to me, when a man enters a woman, a man enters a soul. I really believe that. So last night…"

"You were right."

"Dale…"

"I mean it."

"I wasn't ready to enter your soul. It wasn't right. It would have denied every step we've been taking together."

"Really. You're right. I'm all out of whack. But maybe like, on our first date, instead you should've brought me bowling or something."

"It is kinda crazy."

"What, going off into the woods with a total stranger and spending the whole day naked together? First date?"

He laughs, and okay maybe after last night he thinks I'm a total lunatic, and I don't blame him but me, looking at him? I love this guy. I gotta get my act together here and let him know that. I got some good creative shit to bring to this party. I got shit to offer. If I can just stop acting so wacko around this sex stuff.

He's staring at me as if I'm nuts, "What are you thinking about?"

"Oh, you know, just stuff. Chatter."

I want to get up and get dressed. Meet the day. I unzip the sleeping bag and now I'm like, holy shit, I'm naked and he's standing right there, but he turns and bends to make the coffee and I scoot out and yank on my clothes and I realize how cold it is. I mean, I can see my breath and the beach is damp and still in the shadows.

"I'm freezing."

"Wrap your bag over your shoulders."

"Yessir." And I do as I'm told and it helps.

He hands me a steel mug of dark roast coffee, no milk, no sugar. I sip it and it burns my lips and mouth, strong and bitter and bursting. "Jeez." And we stand there, in front of the fire, at angles to each other. I got smoke all over me.

"Hey, come here. Get out of the smoke."

I walk to him, bare feet in the damp grainy sand, holding my steel mug of coffee, and he's got his coffee in his hand, and so we don't touch, we don't press together, we just lean our heads in, me tilting up, him tilting down, and we kiss. And it is the most beautiful, loving, understanding, gentlest kiss I have ever known.

Then we break apart and pull the pads up around the fire, because it really is cold out and we don't have jackets or sweaters, and the morning sun still hasn't reached the damp beach, so we sit, shifting on the pads, pulling a bag over our shoulders, dodging the smoke, kissing, nuzzling. Feeling the love. And the coffee. My stomach gurgles so loud even I'm embarrassed and usually shit like that doesn't faze me. Emilio laughs.

"If you need to take a dump, there's toilet paper so just go find a private place away from the river, dig a little hole and…"

"I know how to take a dump in the woods, Mr. Ojai."

"Oh. Sorry. Miss Oh–hi–oh."

I laugh, and then suddenly I'm scrambling, my intestines saying, girl, between the chili and the coffee and those little bugs in the water, you better find some place where you can yank down your shorts. Do it! So I'm running up the beach and ducking behind a bush just in the nick of time. Squatting there thinking, Jesus, this is it. This is what it means to be in love.

ᕤᕐ

BACA—

I'm in my studio. I've been here since early morning and now it's almost noon. I've been staring at a blank canvas. It is a practice of mine, but this morning it feels like maybe I'm going crazy. When does an exercise become an obsession? When does meditation slip into isolation? Into lunacy?

126

But I'm no lunatic. At least this I know, I'm too selfish. I enjoy the pleasures of earthly delights far too much to risk losing them. So maybe that's why I'm so bent out of joint about Dale and Emilio. Where are they? Where is she?

❦

EMILIO—

My Pops is a pretty sensitive soul. I know him. So when Dale and I are finally back in the Volvo winding our way down the 33 into Ojai and driving up to his house and walking in, I go neutral, because getting into the masculine thing with him, no way I'm going there. But I can see how happy he is to see us, both of us. And somehow we end up in this three-way hug, and it's good, you know, it gets us laughing and Pops is saying,

"I'm not even gonna ask! I don't wanna know all the crazy shit you two have been through the last 24 hours!"

Dale is full of light, "Baca, you do not want to know."

And I look into my Pops' eyes and I say, "I brought her back, right? Safe and sound."

"I don't know," says Baca, then he turns to Dale, "Are you safe and sound?"

And she smiles and says, "Right here, right now? Yes."

And I say, "See, Pops. I told you. Now I'm outta here."

DALE—

Say what? What does he mean he's outta here? 'Cause I'm thinking all the way back in the car, okay, now we're heading back to civilization, clean sheets and hot water, and I'm picturing how I'm gonna help cook tonight, you know? Be all helpful in the kitchen, feeding my new man, then holding out my hand as he takes me to bed, and I'm promising myself this time I'll go slow, I'll be totally female, I'll cool my jets and just see what he's got to offer, sexually, and I'm imagining all sorts of beautiful stuff, how I'll just lie there and let him bring it to me, like all slow and Zen-Tantra-style as I lay back on the bed, feet dangling to the floor, Emilio on his knees before me as I wait for the first touch of his tongue. But no, suddenly I'm hearing that he's taking off. He's outta here.

He grabs the keys to his van off the side table and nods to Baca as he replaces them with the Volvo keys. Halfway out the door he turns and smiles back at his father.

"You ever get down to Mondo's?"

"I did, actually."

"Put some gas in the van?"

"Yes."

"Get in the water?"

"Yeah, it was nice. That board was perfect."

"The fun-board."

"Yeah."

"That's good then. That's a step, right? Hey, Pops, that's a step?"

"Yeah, that's a step."

"La niña no necesita saber sobre nosotros."

"La niña sabe más que tú y yo combinado."

They smile, then Emilio kisses him on the lips and takes my hand and leads me out to the van and the June sun is overhead and hot, hot off the driveway, and we reach the van and he pulls me against him and kisses me and says,

"This is good for us. A couple days…"

"Where you going?"

"L.A. I've got these friends…"

"L.A.?!"

"Yeah. Echo Park actually. We're gonna hang out, make some music."

I'm absolutely stunned. I'm like, what the fuck!? I come all the way out here to the boonies, right? And I'm paying all these dues to be with this guy and now he's heading down to L.A.!? That's my hood. And he's leaving me here? With his father?!

"You're kidding."

"Uh, no."

I feel my eyes filling with tears, and I don't know what to say. He lifts my chin and kisses me and suddenly he's very forceful with me.

"You don't think I want you. You're uncertain how much I love you and how much I want to make this work. Between us."

"Yes," I say.

"Don't be," and he's all over me, pressing into me, kissing me, wrapping me up. "What's today, Tuesday? I'll be back Thursday. Thursday afternoon. Can we make a date?

"Uh."

"I'll take you out. We'll go out."

And he kisses me again, then climbs into his van, cranks the engine and drives off, yelling back at me as he rolls down the window.

"And don't let the old man pull any funny stuff!"

છ

RANIA—

Why aren't we all the same sex? Wouldn't that be a better design?

છ

EMILIO—

Leaving Ojai, bombing down Foothill, then reminding myself the local cops have their eyes out for young longhairs driving vans. I slow down, cut through the Arbolada and gently merge where the avenue hits the 33, then I settle into a nice easy cruise to Los Angeles to get a little peace and quiet. Go figure. My brain is swirling. I don't have a handle on this. I think of Dale and I immediately feel her, physically she just rushes right through me, but now I'm thinking, what do I know about her? Why am I so captivated? Because Baca is? Rania? Just taking their word that she's some brilliant artist? What's in this for me? This girl is messed up. Now I know it first hand, but instead of gently hardening to her and slowly backing away like I should, my heart is plunging into her.

My heart wants to be with her.

So why am I driving away? Because love, this love, is too important not to test it. To step away from it.

And hey, maybe the old man's got a shot at straightening her out a bit while I'm gone.

❦

BACA—

Straighten her out? I'm just trying to provide some basic needs here. I make her a quesadilla with some crème fraiche and killer salsa and she devours it. I bring her a glass of lemonade and she gulps it down. She's boiling over with tension, exhilaration. Staring at me, staring into space.

I touch her face and look into her eyes and smile. "We don't need to say a word. I know you need some time. Come with me."

I lead her outside, around the pool, under the arbor to a chaise lounge. I brush off the fallen wisteria petals and she stretches out and lays her head back.

"Why don't you just be quiet here in the shade. Have some quiet time."

"Okay."

"I can bring you a pad and charcoal. You can draw a bit."

"What?"

"You're an artist, right? So I was thinking maybe you'd like to draw a bit."

"Oh. Sure."

"You're all spaced out."

"What?"

So I leave her alone, and the afternoon drifts away. Me looking out there from time to time—first, she's sleeping, soundly. And later she's tossing. I give it a while and look again and now she's sitting up, drawing, her face all screwed up. Then, late into the afternoon, I look out to see her sleeping again, so I stroll out and walk up to her and lift the sketchpad and look.

She draws a picture of Rania and me. It is very intimate—raw and disturbing. It is a drawing from inside my bedroom, when Rania and I were all sexed up, Rania sitting naked on the bed, and me, standing in the doorway of the bathroom. I remember this moment vividly. The night when Rania and I—through story—invited Dale into our bed. And we each had our way with her. Fantasy, yes? We are in fantasy. So how can she know this? This picture, so perfect in detail?

But of course she was there. Of course she watched us, and participated and remembers.

I place the drawing back down on the table and walk away.

By evening, it is gone from the sketchbook.

By nighttime this young witch Dale and I are naked together in the hot tub. It is not sexual, but again everything is sexual. So here I am, the mighty Baca, me too, under her spell. This beautiful, complicated, talented ball of creativity and life. The water is hot, steaming, just enough that you must rise out of it every few minutes.

Dale is fired up after her night in the Sespe with Emilio. Brimming over with energy after several naps and a hearty risotto and two glasses of Merlot. It's late, almost midnight, but she's alive as can be. Looking up at the stars. Getting all metaphysical on me.

"We're a ball in space," she says.

"Yes," I say.

"No, I fucking mean it—we're this tiny little marble spinning around in this huge universe."

"Yes," I say.

We keep staring at the stars and it is remarkable, yes? When you look. And imagine. I say, "To me, at my deepest, there is only one question." I look to her, this young girl, and I know there is a reason I'm hanging in with her. Because I am selfish, remember? And I know that somehow, she has something to offer me.

She keeps staring at the night sky through the rising steam.

"What?" she asks.

"It's this," I say. "And it may be about god and it may not. To me it's physics. Does the universe curve back in on itself? Is there a limit to it? Or does it keep on going, forever and ever? In every direction."

"Don't be dumb," she says. "It curls back in. That's all. That's all we have."

"How are you so sure?"

"Because the other way, it's too much. Going off in every direction? Forever and fucking ever? That's too much."

But I know she's wrong. Off course it's too much to consider, and with the certainty of youth, she chooses sanity. While I? I am cursed with the belief of the unbelievable, the incomprehensible. There are some nights, as I contemplate existence, that I fear the fear I feel will stop my heart.

As we stare into space. Get our breathing in sync. Considering.

"So what's the deal about God?" she asks.

"You want my take?"

"Yeah."

I settle deeper into the hot tub. I feel the brush of her foot on my calf.

"God is the brush of your foot on my calf."

"What?"

"What? What did I say?" I stare at her. I am in a pleasant fog. A couple glasses of wine, the heat of the water. The intoxication of this naked young woman.

"You're drunk," she laughs.

"No, I'm not. Here, I'll prove it." And now suddenly I'm scooting up in the hot tub, lifting myself onto the redwood deck, my skin steaming in the cool night. And I know I'm exposing my penis to her, so of course I know its condition. Through all the bullshit, every man, in every situation, knows the shape of his dick, and if he's exposing it, like me, here and now, he's acute about it. Acutely aware. And my dick, right now, with the help of the steaming water and the sex in the air, my dick is doing okay for itself. And so I continue,

"Here's my take on God. Before there was anything, there was only God. And God was lonely, so in one desperate moment, God pulled all his power and force and energy together and—BAM!!!—God shot his entire wad. All in one shot, like fourteen billion years ago. The big bang. And then God retired. I'm done, he says. That's all I'm good for. You're on your own."

Dale stares up into the skies. "Okay," she says. "So God shot his wad. And that's it?"

"That's it."

I slip back into the water, thinking, she just might want to make love with me and what will I do with that? With the basic push and pull of energy between us—feminine to masculine. Forgetting Emilio. Living only for the moment. And me, with that little speech, feeling all manned up, and then I look over and see she's falling asleep. What the fuck? Falling asleep on me. And that was some of my best stuff.

RANIA—

I am sorry, but I know what's going on. With Emilio, with Baca. With Dale. My love for her yearns to be in her presence, but it's the men who are winning this fight. Both of them. Controlling all the action in that way of theirs. Controlling Dale, from close and afar.

I'm in turmoil. There's no more denying it.

Completely out of balance. My desire for Dale suddenly the quicksilver for me—the focal point of all that is still wrong in my life. My relationship to men, to women, to this existence itself that I pretend to sashay through, when in reality, I am just one more mortal soul, sucked into some crazy love vortex of another's being.

But I am full of piss and vinegar tonight, so look out.

Dale, she's on her own.

And me?—me too. There's some event at Bergamot Station—a celebration of young artists and Bill asked me to come, weeks ago, and just now I'm remembering, and I am thinking, sure, why not? I'm on the prowl here. And I know who I'm looking for. I slowly strip and shower and dry and lotion and find a red silk shirt and leather skirt, leaving my legs bare, and with my hair a mess I decide to push the envelope, so I cover my head with a beautiful hijab, direct from Beirut, and that combined with my heels and black leather jacket I grab just in case—I ask anyone not to be intrigued.

In seventeen minutes I'm cruising into the Bergamot lot and parking the Mercedes and walking in my heels towards a rather thin crowd. It throws me off guard. I imagined the entire lot would be packed with young bodies, vibrant young artists, running from gallery to gallery, their proud parents milling about, the whole Venice group there to show solidarity with

134

these kids, but instead the vibe is cool and discombobulated. Low turnout. Night time fog creeping all the way past 26th Street.

I reorient myself. There are bodies moving in my periphery and I know I must join them. But it's the smell of him that gets me. I can smell this guy and then I spot him, in the gap leading to the gift shop where they've set up a makeshift bar, and he's working it, and there are some kids milling about, but I can tell from his body language that he's not happy. The low turnout. The fog. The kids who don't drink alcohol and the parents who don't drink in front of their kids, so it's a zero tip night, and he's bored and pissed off from pouring too many free Cokes and now what does he have? Me.

Right in his face.

"I'll have a Vodka cranberry."

He smiles, "Yeah?"

"Yeah." And I'm staring at this young man, and I have a serious itch to scratch. I stare harder. I try to stare into his soul but he's not letting me anywhere close. But still, I know this is the man who fucked Dale, right here on this lot, on a night like this, stealing her away into the shadows and pushing her up against the chain link, just like she asked for it, and pulling up her dress and pulling down her panties and forcing himself into her. It was this man. This young man standing in front of me, and I'm thinking, maybe you will have me just like you had her. Maybe right now, tonight, I will have you just like she had you.

My cunt squeaks with the thought of it. Maybe that's why I am here. I stare into his soul.

"Do you remember me?" I ask.

He stares at me.

"A few days ago, my young friend and I, at lunch. We ordered sandwiches."

"Uh…"

135

"You didn't acknowledge who she was. Remember? She's young and tall, short dark hair? Her name is Dale. We ordered sandwiches… you don't remember?"

"Listen…" he says.

"No," I say. "You listen. On a night just like this, you pushed her up against the chain link fence, right there, that fence, and…"

"And what?!"

"And you fucked her. Just like that."

And that fast he's around the bar and bullying right up into me, his face gone all crazed and he's talking right into my eyes, low and mean, "Lady, don't fuck with me here. I'm trying to make a buck and maybe a connection or two, so whatever your shit's about tonight, it's not about me. Get it? It's not about me."

I turn on my high heels and stride away. I am not a fool. I know both evil and danger. This young man is not evil, he's too stupid for that. But he is dangerous. So I stride off, filled with piss for men.

❧

EMILIO—

I'm at my friend Patrick's, a whole bunch of us, in his funky little house on a hill in Echo Park and he affords it by reselling weed from his medical marijuana card, and he's got this prescription for Adderall that's bringing in another seventy-five bucks a week or so, and he's a cool guy, and a very talented musician, so it's nice, you know, to be able to crash here, and make some music, but tonight there's an ill wind somehow, maybe some of the cats he invited over, and I'm worried about the vibe and how a couple of these guys are eyeing our guitars, and I'm like, I'm ready to be outta here, and just then this chick who's been all to herself all night, she's suddenly coming up to me asking,

"Hey, can you get me home?"

I say yes, and that quick I'm out the door, guitar in hand, and my wallet and keys and phone in the pockets of my jeans—me patting for them—and this girl on my arm, and she's sweet, and as we're bouncing down the outside stairs I see the sway of her hips, the round of her ass, and I'm bringing it all in, considering the possibilities, but really for me, tonight, with Dale so first in my mind, this girl, she is nothing but an angel. She just saved me from getting boosted by some criminal assholes. I drive her in the van, and she actually lives in a not so bad hood, just below Melrose, south of Paramount Studios, sharing a house with some girlfriends with bars on the windows and everything, so I lock the van on the street and follow her inside. We don't make love. We hardly even kiss. She finds me a toothbrush and I brush my teeth, and nod hi to some sleepy roommate, and I crawl into bed with her with my clothes still on, and I can tell that for her this is perfect. Because she's delicate. Like all women. And tonight to have someone get her home safe, and hold her, and sleep with her, that makes her happy and it works for me too.

❧

BACA—

So how do you get a naked girl out of the hot tub when she's so sleepy her legs are like rubber? It is not so easy. But of course with Dale, it is my greatest pleasure. To dry her and wrap a towel around her in the cool air then walk her inside, the stupid pea gravel sticking to our feet, but she doesn't care and neither do I. Inside to bed, wiping the gravel off her soles as her wet head hits the pillow. I cover her up, turn out the light and close the door as I leave.

RANIA—

I drive through the fog and make it back to my high-rise apartment building at the end of San Vicente. At every stoplight, I am alert for predators, even knowing my car doors are locked. And as I stick my card into the gate pass, I am looking in my mirror, feeling at my most vulnerable. Vulnerable to who? To what? To men.

To some man.

Some man out there who has it in for me.

Like the moron at Bergamot tonight. And now I'm not thinking of me, I'm thinking of Dale. This guy didn't even remember Dale, and it kills me how she let this cretin stick his dick in her, fuck her like that, up against the fence, then not even remember her?! Not even remember her name.

It's killing me here, me, hurrying through the underground garage, waiting for the elevator, looking around, alert then finally safe in the elevator as my tears finally come, tears for all the women, all the girls.

I'm feeling it for all of us, over all time, all those who have suffered at the hands of men, I am crying out for all of us, girls and women, who deserve better. No more with the guy at the bar with the fancy talk and attitude. No more with him. No more with the asshole in Pakistan who kills a girl for going to school. No more with the asshole in Nigeria who cuts off a girl's clit in the name of god. No more with the sanctimonious asshole from Missouri who's going to control my uterus. No more with these men! These men who push and push and force us into servitude and crush our spirits and ridicule our dreams. These men who we know, deep in our hearts, we women know, are so pitiful and insecure in themselves, and how we can be so there to help them be the men they can be if they would only let us, but instead they slap us down. Filled with fear. These fucking scaredy-cat men. You stupid, chickenshit motherfuckers, and how you then fuck with women and girls, how fucking dare you turn your personal failings on us?! How dare you?! These men who should suck dirt. You, men, you who were born of women. Remember that? You fucking cocksuckers? You came out of your mother's cunt, and she paid a price to see you born! Remember that? Of course not! All these motherfucking men, so afraid to face themselves. These men who hate their mothers. These men, these men...and on a night like tonight, I say, fuck them all, these men. Fuck them all. And in my darkest hour, I imagine reversing the tables. I can get the knives out, believe me, in my darkest moment, we can go to the knives, and maybe we should. Maybe it's come to that. In some places at least. But really, I'm just trying to make a point. Truly, I am quieting down here. I'm catching my breath. I'm making this appeal. To all the men out there. Leave us alone, okay? Unless you're going to be respectful. Leave us the fuck alone.

☙

BACA—

Boy, does Rania have a hair up her ass tonight or what?

☙

DALE—

Don't ask me. I'm totally zonked out on clean sheets in Baca's guest room with pea gravel between my toes and all my chakras off to sleep like a string of seven little puppies. So don't get me involved with this. I'm sleepy.

EMILIO—

And me? I'm spooning some girl I don't even know, and that's how it happens when you're twenty-three, and it's not about anything else but what it is, a simple Hollywood hook-up, safe and sweet in its own way, both of us near sleep, and when she takes my hand and moves it to her breast and I feel the instant twitch of my dick, I'm thinking, no, no, I'll enjoy this moment, sure, the feel of her beautiful breast, but no more, and that's how we leave it, me falling asleep with this strange girl in my arms when all I can think of is Dale.

Dale the angel. Dale the witch. Dale the one who wore me out, wrung me out, drove me away, knowing I'd come back. She knows that. Good for her.

ᘒ

DALE—

What the fuck is this guy talking about? I mean I'm half asleep, but I'm serious. I mean, like twenty-four hours ago I had his fucking dick in my mouth, all right?—and right now, now he's falling asleep with some chick in Hollywood, and I'm realizing I'm going nowhere with this, that it's meaningless, really, in the big picture, and then my stupid brain starts reminding me like, well weren't you just naked in a hot tub with his father, and now you know, I know I'm done. I am lost. I am toast.

But it still feels good. Like maybe I'm getting someplace. With Emilio, with Baca. And Rania? Yeah, her too, shaking her free of me. To each his own.

EMILIO—

As intense as it is between me and Dale, I'm realizing, hey, I'm having a meaningful moment here in Hollywood. This girl and me. It isn't about love, it's not like that. It's the exchange of energy, there's like this nice relaxed profound understanding between us, the feminine and the masculine, that she and I provide for each other. On this night. But still, as I drift off into sleep I'm haunted.

I'm out of integrity.

∾

RANIA—

I finally fall asleep thinking I am glad to have that crazy man-rant out of my system. And I awake in a peaceful place.

I love men.

∾

BACA—

Wednesday. Hump day. I wake up thinking, God, if this is your plan, can you blame me for wondering what you've been smoking? I'm serious. Look at this situation. Or, you know what? Don't. Screw it. I'm not gonna analyze this. Here's my plan.

When Dale wakes up, I will lead her through a purely magical day. A day that I orchestrate for her, that I offer her, not just for her but for all of us, Rania, Emilio and me too—it's a clarity that sometimes comes over me, how I can control a situation, I can give people their own strength, no? And it takes something out of me, but it gives back to me in return. So here

141

we go—totally in balance, never allowing her shadow side to question me, to throw at me the monkey wrench that keeps messing her up inside. So none of that.

I am in charge here. I am Baca.

∽

DALE—

Who can say no when yes means so much?

I first heard that from my crazy grandmother back in Ohio. She had oatmeal on her chin you know, and I was the only one who'd listen to her. And I'm remembering it because I get up and I'm like, what the fuck is going on here?— here's this guy Emilio who I'm totally over the moon about, okay? I mean, over the moon, so he's skipped out and here I am with his father.

And instead of fighting it? I'm like, whatever…

BACA—

That's what I want from her. Whatever. Because she is always lashing out, this one. Kicking up the heels. And this is not about men controlling women, and Rania will be with me on this…

RANIA—

I am actually.

∽

BACA—

Okay, so here we go. As I hear Dale coming down the hall, I suck up all my positive energy and envelope her in a love field. It is irresistible to her. Another trick, but it comes from my heart. So immediately we are laughing and joking around about how I am Mr. Fixit—as we head to the studio and without a word she strips out of her clothes and lies down on the massage table, yes? So there she is as the morning sun streams in.

I put on some music, light some incense, squirt oil in my hands and rub them together to make it warm. And then I go to work on her. Working first her fingers, hands, her arms. Then her toes, her feet, her legs. And I can feel the change in her body, finding only a few knots, finding her muscles and her flesh not so much fighting.

I say, "So, Emilio, he was good for you, yes?"

She doesn't answer. Instead a mean growl comes out of her throat and I think, whew, we still got some work to do here. And as I massage her I begin talking, "Our lives have bad things. Trauma. Every one of us. Some people deny it and live a life of lies. And other people make it bigger than it really is, yes? And so they are in a constant neurotic state. Or you can explore it—in small bits, with a guide, or maybe two. I don't know. But by exploring, you don't let that trauma tell you who you are. You tell it who you are."

"Yeah," she says. "Whatever."

I'm not sure how to take that.

I work my way up the backs of her thighs, spreading more oil, then working my fingers into the flesh of her ass, letting her know by my touch that I have no sexual interest in her at this moment, although the scent of her, and the glimpse of her crack, the two openings, suddenly makes my penis jump, and that makes me smile, as I say to it—Oh, good morning. Nice of you to join us, finally.

But, Dale, she is with me, she is in total relaxation until I begin moving up from her ass to the small of her back, where she has two dimples, the most magical of symbols in a woman's back, but before I can get to them, as I am moving up towards

143

her base chakra, at the tip of her spine, just above the anus, her whole body goes tense.

"Ahh! Fuck! Jesus, Baca!"

"Easy," I say. "Easy. What?"

"Ow!"

"Oh. Sorry." And then I feel it, wrapping around her tailbone, a knot, a knot like a rope tied around her base chakra. Tense and tender. I have never felt anything like this. It makes itself so obvious to me now. So I begin to work around it, slowly, my fingers gently probing, as I make my breathing bigger, yes? Deeper and louder until Dale falls into the breathing with me. She is learning.

As I work the area, I go into some more talk—and even for myself, how much I believe it, I do not know. But I figure if some very enlightened dudes in India came up with this stuff, it is at least worth looking into. And also me, when I feel powerful like this, I could read her the phone book and it would work.

Anyway, I say, "So the Hindus, three thousand years ago, they discover chakra. Energy centers. And for artists, like you and me, this is important. Your base chakra, centered by the asshole, here is where your kundalini comes from. The creative spirit. And it is dying to express, yes? It must express itself. So it begins to rise, up your spine, to your next chakra—the sex chakra. And this is immediately a very powerful mix of energy. And for the artist, this is where we get stuck, because suddenly all that pure creative energy, kundalini, we are expressing it through sex, and so we do this, but then what? The kundalini retreats to the base chakra, when actually it should keep rising, up your backbone, higher into your consciousness, but instead, you lose your art. You are stuck."

"So essentially you're saying you don't want me fucking Emilio."

I laugh. Where does this girl come up with this shit? Then I remember that maybe she is a witch.

"Dale, sex can elevate your art. And Emilio, he is the perfect partner for you. But what do you have to offer in return?"

"I..."

"Ssshhh. Think about it."

I can give up to her no power today. None. That is my task.

❧

EMILIO—

Down in Hollywood, in a buttoned up little house on a side street. As we climb out of bed, me and this girl whose name I do not know, I see her more clearly in the morning light, and she really is lovely. A sensitive soul, and I feel her telling me with her eyes and her body that she wants me and I remember something my Pops told me the day I turned eighteen—"Any chance you have to make love to a woman, do it."

I smile to myself remembering and this girl whose name I do not know takes my smile for something else, and she opens her body to me, subtly, but she puts it out there. And then we have to go through that delicate dance of denial—saving face, because for a woman to offer herself only to be turned down, that causes a deep hurt. If it wasn't for Dale, I don't know, I don't know. We kiss, this girl and me, and I'm out the door.

❧

RANIA—

This is a hard day for me. Psychologically. Today, I cannot be helped by Eastern philosophy. Massage. Candles and incense? Not today. I need a shrink. A good shrink and a stiff drink. I'm a mess.

145

DALE—

Every time I show resistance, Baca finds a way. He makes me laugh. Then he gets all defensive. Whatever it takes, this guy is running the show and that's okay by me.

I can think only of Emilio. My mind goes day-tripping back to the Sespe. I am a swirl of images and memories, the smell of him, his touch. And then a flood of insecurity. Am I worthy? I'm all fucked up here. Maybe Baca was onto something when his hands on my back made it hurt so much. Too much for this girl, and he knew it, so we walked back down the path and he had me make him lunch, him all bossy and shit, but that felt right to me. He's dropping all this energy into me, and by now I trust him, I really trust him.

And so the afternoon slides into evening, and it's warm and peaceful and I have this amazing man telling me how beautiful I am, how talented, and then poking at me, like, well, what about this? When are you willing to get down to this? And I'm not willing, and I let him know, and he's so kind saying, you will be, you will, because you are an artist. You are a lover. But you can't get there from here on a flat tire.

"That's it?! My whole fucked up past—to you it's a flat tire?"

"Yeah, and I got the jack."

"You got jack-shit, Baca. Come on."

Whew, wrong thing to say. He goes stone cold silent until I say, "Hey, Baca, hey."

Then he zeroes in on me, "I am here to serve you, but not to be disrespected."

And now I'm knowing what Emilio meant when he said how Baca can makes things so fucking uncomfortable. I'm squirming here. I'm like a fish on the line, all through dinner, him being all distant, and I'm feeling bad about it, because really, what's in it for him? I mean it. What's in it for Baca? Me all moony for his son. Rania all fucked up about things... and here he is, this Peruvian with the black hair and black eyes, putting out for me. Trying to help me. I want to cry. I want to make it right. I know he's helping me, and I want to make things right.

We get through dinner kind of quiet, doing the fragile thing. I'm so filled with love for him. But I'm faltering, I've lost strength. Then this strange thing happens, we've finished eating, still at the table, and underneath I've got my right hand holding onto my left, okay? Just unconscious like. And then I start squeezing the base of my left thumb, and suddenly the memory comes back to me, the same memory, my highest moment, when I rode out on that bus from Ohio. And I'm filled with this sudden calm and power, and it's not like the old me getting all bustered up about something. It's calmer. What Emilio taught me, it's working. And suddenly I'm feeling the power to regain my footing. To make things right.

"Hey, Baca..."

"Yes?"

"What can I do for you?"

He thinks for a long time. I mean like two or three minutes which really, when things are tense, that's a long fucking time.

Finally he says, "You know."

"No. What? What?"

"You know. In our dreams tonight, this can be your gift to me."

And suddenly I know what he means and my body flushes with heat and hormones or something. But it's not even sexual, and that's part of what I'm learning here too, how you can get these flushes, these like whole body rushes that go beyond to where it's reaching a deeper place.

147

BACA—

What is it? This bung-hole kundalini obsession of mine. Maybe it is because I am a painter, I don't know. Or maybe because the Hindu ancients were onto something. Or maybe because my mother was Catholic. I don't know.

DALE—

We finished a bottle of wine and when my wino self went looking for another, Baca said, no. We'll drink some water. So I drank a glass of water and we hugged goodnight. I went off to my room and ran a hot shower. I stripped out of my clothes and took a long look at myself in the mirror. I could see I was changing. I'm looking right into my own eyes. Then I stare down my body and I like what I see. Why? Maybe because now I know how Emilio likes it. And Baca. And Rania. Maybe now I'm liking it more myself.

I put one foot up on the counter alongside the sink and looked down on my pussy. I spread my lips a bit, staring at my sex, remembering the mirror work I did with Rania, it seems like weeks ago. So much has happened. I step into the streaming water and soap myself everywhere, knowing what I am offering to Baca. Squeaky clean, the girl from Ohio.

So here I am, stepping out, my skin all flushed, the night still warm as I dry off and pull on my beautiful white nightgown. I click off the bathroom light and step into the bedroom and walk to the bed. I feel like I'm in a trance. I know that right now, I should be filled with love and lust for Emilio, but instead, tonight, it is Baca I am here for. My friend Baca. I turn off the lamp on the night table. A cool white light spills through the window onto the white down comforter. The moon I guess.

I climb onto the bed and lie down across it. I am hot and cool. Filled with this strange energy that I do not understand.

I feel my back, my ass, my legs pressing into the smooth comforter. I make an effort to control my breathing. Then I reach down with my hands and I raise my hips off the bed, and I pull up my nightgown. Up over my thighs, my hips, my ass.

I spread my legs and I lay there quietly. My offering now. My offering to Baca. And he can have whatever he wants. I'm not some stupid girl in the woods. Not someone else's fantasy. This is my fantasy. My gift to my teacher. But he doesn't come.

So I roll onto my side, my nightgown still pulled up over my hips and wait, and wait, but he does not come. Ten minutes go by. Twenty. An hour. I'm half-asleep, almost dreaming, then suddenly I know. So I roll over onto my stomach, making sure my nightgown is still pulled up high. Face down on the bed, I spread my legs further and stick my feet up like some teenage girl. I might as well be wearing bobby socks. Maybe I am as I slip into sleep.

The quick click of the bedroom door. I feel him, Baca, his manliness, his artfulness, and then I feel his hot breath running up the backs of my thighs, on my ass cheeks and now he's kissing me there, spreading my cheeks with his fingers, and I can feel his lips, wet on my ass, kissing me, then biting me, sharp little bites into the flesh of my ass, his white teeth, again and again, making his mark, bringing my blood to the surface, and then he's kissing my asshole, and then his tongue, entering, pushing deeper. And me just lying there, allowing him, allowing him. Suddenly I feel this powerful burst of my old self, this pissed off girl ready to say, give me more, give me all of it if that's what you want, fuck me there if you want, go for it man! Go for it! But there's something new in me. My right hand grabs for my left. I want to feel free. Feel in control. I know this sounds really weird but it's true, because suddenly instead of getting all angry and yelling, now it's like, because I have something deeper going on, finding a new place for myself, that I can lift my head up and look back at Baca, his face cradled between my cheeks, his tongue in my ass, his eyes filled with light.

"You can do more, Baca. If you want." My voice is steady, quiet. "Put a finger in my ass. Two fingers. You can enter me there if you want. We can find some oil and you can come inside me."

"Ssshh," he says to me. "Girl, you're dreaming. Go back to sleep. It's all a dream."

And with those beautiful words of love and trust and safety and the thrust of his warm wet tongue into my ass, I experience this incredible burst of chakra energy, this energy bursting up from down there, busting out, rushing up my spine, waking all those other chakra puppies up, bing, bing, bing, bing, bing, bing until this white light liquid spiral is shooting up and down my spine, my body, filling me everywhere. And it's not sexual. That's the weirdest part about it. It's deeper. It's weird, it's fucking weird. I'm totally sure this anal stuff is not for everyone, but for me, tonight, and for Baca, a couple of wacko artists, it's our gift to each other. His lips, his tongue. My ass.

Our dreamy little secret.

&

EMILIO—

Me, I'm out of alignment. The whole day, I can't find my rhythm. I drive the van down to Venice to take in the scene, see if the beach break is working 'cause I got my boards in the back, but the parking situation is a mess, and somehow today for me, this mass of humanity all crushing together, looking for some action, looking for connection, it's feeling desperate to me, I don't know, it's all feeling out of joint, and maybe it's after last night, I mean, not even being sexual with that girl, but it's still about that, because really, I know this, deep in my heart, I was out of integrity last night.

I was out of integrity.

Because of my feelings for Dale. Even though it's so young between us, so early with her, it's simple. I shouldn't have been with anyone else. And then I'm thinking, ease up, man, you were just testing it, testing this love you feel, and you passed, you fucking passed, and that should be a comfort, right? I'm okay here. That's a comfort. But I'm still feeling crazy you know why? Because it's Dale I've fallen in love with and she scares me. And that's why I've been down here mucking around in L.A.

I'll sleep in the van north of Malibu. Maybe up in Sycamore Canyon. No way I'm heading back to Ojai tonight. No way. I'm not due back 'til tomorrow and that's when I'll show up. But I'll crash tonight knowing that tomorrow I'm going up to dance the dance. Whatever she's bringing my way, I'm gonna match her.

I love her.

RANIA—

I love her too.

BACA—

Me three. And I just had my tongue in her ass.

RANIA—

Baca!

⁓

DALE—

Baca and me are in the kitchen the next morning. He made coffee. And he's got a hunk of some hard cheese out and a loaf of black bread and I'm thinking, girl, they do not call this breakfast in Ohio. I sit down across from him in this little nook, and the sun is streaming through the windows, and I've got the smell of coffee and black bread and cheese in my nose and I don't know what's real and what's a dream anymore.

Especially about last night.

Baca stares into my eyes.

I stare deep into his.

He stares deeper into mine.

I stare deeper into his—both caught up in the dream of last night. Until finally I say,

"Let me see your tongue."

And then we laugh. Laugh and laugh.

BACA—

And there she did it again, see? This girl, she's a witch, but maybe she's a good witch. Or maybe she's just witchy, I don't know. And I guess that's part of the magic here, and for her to bring me into her dream last night, that was good of her. But look, it's Thursday and change is in the air.

Today Emilio returns.

❦

EMILIO—

Man, I'm too sensitive. I'm not talking about love, I'm just talking about the morons at the next campsite over, and all the generators banging away, I mean what the fuck, you're out here in Sycamore Canyon, and it's still rugged, still holding its own with the Pacific pounding in on the beach, straight across PCH, so you come out here for a little peace and quiet, but you people bring all your shit with you. I don't know. Sometimes my friends and me, we just start feeling so crowded, so hemmed in, but I love Cali. I love it here. But now I'm thinking of heading back down to Peru, or just going off on this prolonged journey somewhere. I don't know.

I shake my head clear and face my reality. The reality of Dale.

I'm wary of her, but I want her. I need her. But I'm trying to visualize the fit, you know? What kind of fit can we make?

And I'm seeing us traveling the world together, and she brings me into art and I bring her into the ocean, and then suddenly I'm thinking about kids, like if I ever want to have kids, I want Dale to be their mother. A woman with that kind of fire.

Not the most rational choice in the world I know. I know. But that is the mystery of Dale.

I drive back to Ojai.

೮ನ

RANIA—

They have hijacked this girl from me, these two men. These two men who I love so deeply. They have hijacked this girl I have fallen in love with. I know the ridiculousness of my situation. The selfishness. You don't have to tell me.

But a passion this strong, no matter its origin, cannot be denied.

೮ನ

DALE—

It's mid-afternoon. Baca's in his studio. I'm in a daze, lying naked out by the pool. This is my newest hobby. Nudism. And in that spirit this morning I found my mirror and some scissors and gave myself a total trim job. In the spirit of nudism. And next time someone asks what I do, I'll say, oh, I'm a nudist.

God, listen to me. The anticipation of Emilio is turning me into an idiot. That and the hot sun and this warm glow in my base chakra, this kinda quiet groove down there that I'm thinking is that about last night? But today's today, and I want him. Emilio. I want to be with him. Then, finally, I hear his van rumbling up the driveway. I stand up deciding what do I do here? Do I get dressed? Pull on my t-shirt and shorts and go meet him? Or just walk out as I am? Naked? Just having some fun with it, laying it out there for him, like Sespe all over, let's cut to the chase here, and suddenly I'm out there in my mind, stark naked as the van pulls in, and I see the look on his face and I'm smiling and shrugging, holding my arms out as he steps out of the van and he's just more rugged and handsome and sensitive and wild and concerned than ever before, and I'm just creaming for him, really, to tell you the truth here, but he's got this smile as he stares into my eyes, then looks down the length of my body, and looks at my sex and says,

"Look at you, you're all trimmed up."

"Yeah. You like it?"

"Yes." And we step together, and he kisses me and presses against me, and puts his hand on my ass and says,

"I think your ass is peeling."

"What?"

And now I'm just glad I'm only imagining this right? But it's kinda scary, like I'm moving into lucid daydreaming now, like, that just happened really, but I know it didn't. I'm still at the pool. So I pull up my shorts and pull on my top and do this hands through my hair thing as if that'll help the least bit, and then I'm heading across the lawn, through the house and out the front door to meet this man I love.

EMILIO—

As she steps outside my heart leaps. And I also feel the deepest part of me flush with warmth, and that's reassuring, you know? Paying attention to those deepest reactions? And I'm out of the van as she rushes into my arms and I lift her, and we kiss, and I turn circles there with her in the driveway, but she's no small woman this Dale, and I'm showing her my strength here, my physical strength, as I clench my chest against her breasts, her feet off the ground and my hand slipping under her shorts, grabbing her ass.

DALE—

And you know what he says? Guess what he says,

"I think your ass is peeling."

And he laughs, and kisses me, but really, now ain't that the shit? Didn't I just live this, like two minutes ago in my mind... didn't I...?

&

BACA—

While me, I'm stewing inside the house. How can I not? I am a man. I am also a father, and I know my son. I know how he is sensitive, but also how he is cold. Me? I did my best with Dale. For him. Because I think they could be good together. But still I am stewing. She needs a few more days. That's what I'm thinking. A few more days with me, and with Rania. And so Emilio coming so fast back into the picture. I don't know.

&

RANIA—

This is unsavory in my mind now. Both these men, they are double-teaming her, and I am out of the picture and I don't like it.

&

DALE—

I do. Now that I'm back in the arms of Emilio. And knowing Baca's got my back. I like it. I feel that Baca and Rania, they have shown me enough. I get it. I'm getting it. Let me rock and roll here, will you please? Let me rock and roll with Emilio.

EMILIO—

And that's what we do. Because today, this day, should feel free and full of love and touch, and I feel by her look and touch that Dale is in the exact same place, and that's how it goes in the glow of this warm afternoon when I have this beautiful girl in my arms, in my orbit, and both of us wanting to kiss, to touch and share skin, but needing to go slow, go slow, go slow.

We jump into the van and I drive her where?—the beach, the mountains? No, we end up at Soule golf course, up on the rise there, east of downtown, and she's like what the…? And I'm saying, let's hit some golf balls, I know it sounds weird, but it's fun, kind of a Zen thing. And before she can object, I grab three clubs outta the bag buried in the back, down under the boards and now just walking through the clubhouse with this girl on my arm, I am the shit. Among these Ojai mooks who keep the whole valley in balance by being Christian and playing golf, I am the shit because of this girl on my arm.

The compliments coming flying my way,

"Hey, surfer-douche-bag, how ya doin'?"

"Yo, Emilio, tell your old man he still owes me twenty for that last back nine."

And I smile back, "Is that your back nine or his back nine?"

And that fast I'm whisking Dale out the other end of the clubhouse, heading for the driving range and she's laughing, "What the fuck was that about?"

"What, that? I've known these guys since I was like three. Two probably. Forever."

"Why?"

"Cause my old man, he's a scratch golfer."

"Baca?"

"Yeah, he never told you that?"

And I don't know what that has to do with anything, but we're having fun, Dale and me, and everyone can feel it. It's a gift we're sharing with everyone around us, so we plug our slugs into the ball machine and of course she's fascinated in some artistic sort of way at how the balls come out of the machine into these metal cage baskets, and they fill up just to the top and that's it, so of course that's fascinating to her, and then we walk up to the tees, and it's warm out, the sun high, but not too hot, and there are maybe seven, eight guys out there, hitting balls, two or three women, a couple of kids, but as we come walking up to an open tee, just feeling so open and smiling and loving, and me with just a three-wood, and two irons, a two and a seven in my hands and her carrying both metal cage buckets of balls like Pollyanna or something, like some Swiss milkmaid and both of us laughing, and everyone's eyes are on us, and that's the way it's supposed to be, right? Young lovers?—spreading the love.

DALE—

So doing something you've never done before, you can take a whack at it, right, or if you're in someone's arms you can just let the energy release. You don't have to even guide it, you can just feel it, and so Emilio, he's not at all bashful about putting a ball up on the little wood thing, then getting up behind me and wrapping his arms around me and gripping the club, his long fingers wrapping over mine, and then after a nice slow backswing the club comes swinging forward and I've got his words in my head, keep your head down, just keep your head down, and it brings a smile and I'm thinking sure if that's all it takes, and then I hear and feel the click of the club hitting the ball and he's suddenly whooping, look, look, lift your head up! And I do and I see this ball flying up, up and away, like past the last yard marker or whatever and I'm like, is that us?!, and he's yelling at me, that's us! That's us!

RANIA—

Let me tell you how it is. For most women, as we reach fifty, as we reach middle-age. It is the saddest thing as you come to realize the diminishment of our sexual urges. It is such a complicated piece of business that no man can truly understand it. The moon, the cycle, the passing from our bodies of the last egg... Even a man like Baca, he can intellectualize that, but he cannot feel that. It is for women to feel. And there is relief in some ways, at first, as if to say, okay, enough then. Enough of that nonsense. Whether you had kids or not. But then it creeps up on you. The realization that your sexuality is slipping away. And me, for one, I will not give up this fight. I cannot let it go. And if it takes a girl like Dale to stir my juices, then so be it.

I am a sexual being and will be until the day I die.

BACA—

Me too. But we are all messed up about sex. We know through Tantra that the highest sex comes from the deepest intimacy. Between two people. But then all that intimacy?— man that shit can get old. And then it's the racy stuff that really gets you going. Like a new partner. Like these two—Dale and Emilio—and the flow of energy between them.

EMILIO—

How good is this feeling to me? Now that Dale and I've got this thing all slowed down we're free. Free to express this love we're feeling. And I know it's mutual. It's in balance. Dale is being beautiful, absolutely beautiful. Loving everything.

We leave the golf course and head downtown to poke around.

℃

DALE—

Walking around Ojai, holding hands, and the sun's this perfect temperature now, and feeling the current, this steady electric current traveling between our two bodies, just through holding hands, it's just filling my body my soul with this deep warm buzzing, and of course he knows everyone, and everyone's saying hello, and he introduces me—"This is my girlfriend, Dale," and him saying that, it just slays me. Kills me.

My knees buckle and I'm flat out on the fucking sidewalk of love, okay?

Somebody call 911.

I have never been happier. Even when I left Ohio, not even then.

Then we're sitting in the grass in the park across from the arcade, watching the little kids on the playground. Emilio leans over and kisses my shoulder. I turn my face to him and he kisses my lips.

"What about dinner?" he says. "We can cook at my place, or we can go out."

"I got some money," I say. "I've got fifty bucks."

"Yeah?"

"Yeah. I found it in my shoe. Had to be Rania. So let's go out. My treat."

"We'll go halfsies. My Pops laid a little cash on me."

"Cool. So maybe you can run me up there."

"What, why?"

"Because we're going out. I gotta get ready. You know. Girl stuff."

"Sorry. No girl stuff."

"What?"

"Hey, really, listen, I love what's goin' on between us."

And here he takes my face in his hands and stares into my eyes and says, "I'm feeling it so deep and natural now, and my old man, you know... maybe he's gonna push you off balance if you go up there."

"Really?"

"Yeah. Maybe he would. I told you he's tricky."

"I wouldn't let him."

"That's right. You won't let him. Because you're not going."

"Really?"

"Yeah. Stay with me. You can take a nap at my cottage."

"Wow, you have a cottage?"

"Yeah, I even have hot water. A shower. On Mallory Way, it's just a couple blocks from here. So that's the plan, and then we'll go have dinner."

For me to have a man now, a real boyfriend, and him taking charge like this, what girl doesn't want this? When you can trust him. Truly trust him. What girl doesn't want this?

We climb back into his van and drive a few blocks then we're pulling off Mallory into this long circular driveway with a whole bunch of cottages scattered around. And there are these tall trees everywhere and it's got a nice vibe. It's quiet. He pulls up alongside a square green cottage with white windows and a dark roof and we climb out and we walk in through the open door.

It's a sweet pad. It's simple, the walls are wood and he's got a couple of nice things around, and it's totally neat and clean, and he's got these Buddhist prayer flags up in the rafters across these skylights, and this nice bed.

I walk through the place, taking it all in, the little kitchen with all these containers of lentils, beans, brown rice, all these different teas and I'm realizing that Emilio, he's really living it, you know? He's living this life people talk about. "This is really cool."

"Thanks. So what do you want first, shower or nap?"

"Nap."

And I lie down on his bed thinking he's gonna join me, but he whispers that he's got some chores, then he pulls this Peruvian blanket over me and kisses my cheek and I'm asleep.

෫෨

BACA—

I'm not calling Emilio. No way. And I'm not calling Rania. And it kind of pisses me off that once again I'm stranded up here on Foothill with my thumb up my ass.

RANIA—

Better his ass than mine.

෫෨

EMILIO—

I'm outside me cottage, cleaning up the van when I hear this shout, "No, no, stop it!" and I rush inside and Dale's on the bed writhing, thrashing, and I grab her, wrap my arms around her saying, hey, hey, and her eyes pop open and all these tears come pouring out. Like a fountain, but she's not sobbing, you know, and her shoulders are totally still, she's perfectly still, her eyes open and I don't even know if she's awake, as she cries this river of tears.

And then she closes her eyes and lies back down and falls back to sleep. It's the strangest thing. Spooky.

DALE—

An hour later I wake up and look around. I'm alone. I'm feeling filled with love and warmth. Anticipation. I step into his tiny bathroom and smell the one towel hanging there. It's clean. I shower and dry myself and wrap the towel around me and as I step back out of the bathroom I'm thinking what, I'm just gonna climb back into the same old shirt and shorts now? And that's how we're gonna go out? But suddenly Emilio's standing there with this nice long-sleeved white cotton tunic thing, like all embroidered and he says,

"Try this on."

I drop the towel and reach for the shirt and hold it up in front of me, and it's big this thing, that soft weave, and I hold it up hiding my body, my face, then I peek over the top at him and make a face like I Love Lucy and he laughs. Then I flip it upside down and pull it on over my wet head and I run my hands through the long sleeves and I feel it fall down over me, my boobs, my belly, my sex, halfway down my thighs. Standing right there in front of him.

"It's nice," I say. "Where'd you get it?"

"At a wedding. Guatemala. Wear it."

"Out? Tonight?"

"Yeah. You look fabulous. *Te miras fabulosa.*"

"You're kidding."

"No."

So I duck back into the bathroom and look in the little mirror and he's right, something about it, it looks really cool. But kinda baggy. I step back out.

"Have you got a belt?"

"Something better." He reaches up into a cupboard and pulls down a spool of nylon cord. He eyeballs me as he unspools

162

a length then slices it with a knife and hands it to me. I wrap it around my waist, bunching the cotton tunic, then tie a bow tie in front. He looks me up and down.

"Do you feel safe in that?"

"Around you, yes."

"You shouldn't."

"Should I wear anything underneath?"

He eyeballs me like I'm some naughty little girl and says sternly, "Yes. We're going out."

❧

EMILIO—

Man, I am hot for this woman. Walking up to Monte Grappa as the sun's dropping low in the sky, strolling out onto the outdoor patio, my arm around her waist, every head turning to look at her. Every one. Because the magic's still working, she and me clicking in perfect rhythm. We share a simple pasta and their cheapest bottle of Chianti and the whole time I'm quizzing her about her art, her life, and she's doing the same with me, filling in the holes, you know. Understanding where we're coming from. And once the food is gone and the sun has set and we're down to our last sips of the dusty wine I lean forward across the table. "Kiss me."

She leans forward and says, "Say my name."

"Dale."

We kiss.

And she says, "Guess what?"

"What?"

"I disobeyed you."

"About?"

"My underwear."

"Liar."

"Wanna bet?" she says. "How about we hold hands under the table?"

We both move our hands under the table, and she takes my hand in hers and guides it between her bare thighs, and she sees people catching glances of her, a waiter in the doorway, staring, and the light's dim with the sun gone but the tables don't have table cloths and so it's hard to have secrets and to Dale maybe, this is her dare, so I just lock eyes with her, and slowly work my hand up between her thighs, up under the white cotton tunic, and as I keep moving up I can feel her subtly shift, opening her legs for me, right there on the restaurant patio, and now I can feel the heat of her sex on my fingers, even before I reach there, I feel it, and I catch the faintest scent of her as I'm wondering what I will find.

I stop, an inch from the answer. I stare into her eyes. She smiles and says,

"So what do I win if I'm right?"

"I take you dancing," I say. She smiles. She laughs.

"And what if you win?"

"I take you back to my cottage and take them off."

❧

DALE—

Earth, Wind and Fire, how about that shit? Earth, Wind and fucking Fire. I'm feeling it, man, here in the Ojai Arts Center on a Thursday night with a few old hippies and a small group of artsy twenty-somethings, everyone doing the Ojai freestyle and there's plenty of room on the dance floor and the lights are dim and the bass is thumping and Emilio's got his groove on. So we dance. We dance til we sweat. We dance and flirt, we dance and grind, and then it's over and we're out the door, and the dry warm air soaks the sweat from our skin.

He grabs me and kisses me, "You know what would taste really good right now? Tequila."

✂

EMILIO—

Big mistake.

Or maybe God works in mysterious ways.

We walk across to Agave Maria's and sit at the bar and the restaurant's emptied out, the busboys cleaning up, you know, with that kitchen clatter and everything, and real quick Dale downs a shot of tequila and orders another, just like a man, like hey, if we're gonna drink, let's fucking drink. And we're laughing and having fun, hands all over each other. And then she looks up into my eyes, and her eyes are so filled with love for me, her soul entering me, filling me, and I'm feeling it, returning it, feeling that yeah, this is it, maybe that really truly she is my love, but then there comes this thing into her eyes, the deepest sadness, right there, sitting at the bar, her in my shirt passing for a dress, and I don't know what to think, wanting only to love her and feel her love in return, but suddenly her eyes are taking it all back, taking back the love she just offered, sucking it all back, her eyes turning black, sucking at mine until I'm afraid, okay? Like she's about to steal something from me, so I turn my head away. I turn away and grab her next shot of tequila and down it. Then I turn back to her.

"You have to tell me."

✂

RANIA—

No she does not. Don't do it, Dale. Don't do it.

BACA—

Rania, who are we to say? Really.

165

EMILIO—

So she tells me, right there at the bar, in this calm flat voice and I hear the midwestern accent, and this story, it's pretty ugly, and I'm not surprised by it, it's what I first picked up on, the first day I met her. When she finishes, I squeeze her hand. And we each have one last shot of tequila and she's quiet, like she's in a trance and I'm feeling such empathy for her, such hurt, but I can see it in her turning it into some quiet rage and I say to her,

"Are you feeling brave right now? You must be."

"Yes," she says.

"Then let's go work this out."

BACA—

What is he thinking here?

RANIA—

I don't know. Maybe he's onto something.

EMILIO—

As we walk into my cottage I know I'm gonna pull some serious magic here. Get her into a state where she can go deep. I'm feeling that we've both got like the perfect mix of tequila and heat and love that we can pull this off, that she can just finally get this shit out of her system. Purge it. I gotta make this happen for her. I'm jazzed about it, my adrenaline's pumping, I can create this vibe for her, sell it to her.

The cottage is still warm, but it's dark. I light a candle. She sits on the edge of my couch. I sit on the corner of my bed, our knees almost touching.

"So I'm seeing that all this pain you went through, that whole thing, that it keeps bringing out this masculine part of you, it makes you want to settle the score, doesn't it?"

"Yeah."

"So come take it. Take it back. Settle the score."

"How?"

"I'll be your guide. So you're back in Ohio, and you're young, your what, eleven, twelve?"

"Eleven."

"And you've got this older step-brother living with you and your mom. No dad around. And this step-brother, he's got these fucked up friends and they start teasing you, right? That's what you told me. They start teasing you and calling you Mary, right? So what was that about? Tell me."

"I told you."

"Tell me again."

"The movie."

"What movie?"

"*There's Something about Mary*, you know."

"Yeah, so what about it? It's about when he came in her hair right? It's about that. And she's walking around with this gob of cum in her hair, what's her name?"

"Cameron Diaz."

"So it's about that."

"Yeah, it's about that. Because they all want to fuck me, right, and they want me to give them blow jobs, and I'm fucking eleven, okay? I'm this kid and they know deep down they can't fucking rape me, right? They can't do that to me. But they can Mary me."

"And they do."

"Yeah. Like every day after school. Again and again."

"And you never told anybody."

"Never."

I let go of her hand and walk to the bathroom and return with a bottle of lotion.

"I'm offering you something tonight, Dale. You can take it, you can own it, but just for tonight, okay? And then you have to give it back to me because it's not yours, it's mine."

"Okay."

I put the lotion down then step out of my clothes and lie naked on my bed.

"Come over here. Come over here and lift your shirt and sit on top of me, straddle me with your legs apart."

She moves almost like a zombie. My penis is soft as she raises the tunic up and settles her crotch down over me. I can feel the brush of her naked vagina on me, her bare thighs against mine. I tell her, scoot down a bit, and she does, exposing me. I stare into her eyes.

"Follow my lead, then when I tell you, you take over. Okay?"

"Okay."

I reach for the lotion and squirt some into her palms.

"Make me hard," I say. She takes my penis in one hand, slippery with lotion and I begin to grow. She slowly strokes it as I grow thicker, longer. And I begin talking to her in a low voice.

"Now you are holding your own masculine. It's in your hands now, this part of you and you're feeling what it's like, aren't you? Feeling the masculine self that lies inside you."

"Yes," she says.

And my dick grows long enough now for both her hands and she begins stroking it, bringing it to its full length, full size, as I keep talking,

"Look down. Look at it. Look at your dick in your hands, feel the power of that. If you feel it, use it use it!"

"Yes."

And now she's stroking me faster, harder, as I see her face scrunching up, her eyes tightening, her breath quickening, and then she's squeezing, squeezing for release, and as I lie there under her I suddenly flush with something new, something feminine coursing through my body, and I realize she's pushing all that onto me, her feminine, turning me into a woman, and her incredible juice is suddenly rushing through me and bringing me into a place so different, me not expecting this, and I'm so lost now in the fantasy, with this feminine energy and looking up at Dale riding me, holding this throbbing erection in her hands this beastly man riding me and I want only to lean forward and take him in my mouth. This is the feminine lust I feel right now and it is scaring me. What is she doing to me?

I fight the urge. I fight for control. This is supposed to be her fantasy, not mine. This is her time. I get a handle on my breathing as she rides me harder, her hands stroking her dick faster and faster and I finally grab the reins back, once again directing the action as I start riffing at her, "They called you Mary, the fucking shitheads, so I lined them up for you, all in a row, all grown men by now, and they're crying, they're afraid, the little shits and I've made them bow their heads and now you can give it back to them, do it, come, come, squirt your cum all over them, do it, Dale, do it! Fucking show them what it feels like! Show them what it feels like!"

"I will! I will!"

"What do you want to do?!"

"Fuck them! Fuck them!"

"Do it then! It's them you want to fuck. It's them you want to humiliate! It's not some poor girl bent over a tree trunk, it's them! It's them! Cum on them! Fuck them up!"

❧

RANIA—

This is dangerous. He should not be doing this.

BACA—

I'm going down there.

RANIA -

It's too late.

∾

DALE—

And suddenly my penis explodes in my hands, and this incredible rush rushes up my spine as there's cum squirting, flying through the air, feeling my cum flying through the air, jerking it, jerking it, spasm after spasm more cum, shooting up out of my balls, shooting through my penis, exploding, exploding… and then, I don't know.

I don't know.

EMILIO—

I know.

Her eyes rolled back into her head and she passed out.

And me covered with my own cum like, what the fuck. Looking over at Dale, slumped over on the bed, fetal, and I can barely hear her breathing, right? She's like catatonic. I roll off the bed and walk around the cottage. I wet a washrag and sponge the cum off my face, my chest. I get dressed. I check her again. Same deal, her eyes open but no response and now I'm worried. I find my cell and call my Pops.

∾

BACA—

This hot June night is now cool. I am at the door as Emilio's van pulls up. It is very late. I have already called Rania and she is on her way.

"Pops…"

"I don't want to hear it."

Dale is sitting in the front seat of the van. I open the door. She stares straight ahead. Her legs and feet are bare, and she has the Peruvian blanket wrapped around her. I reach and take her hand and she steps down from the van and I lead her past Emilio and into the house.

"Pops…"

"Go home," I tell my son.

An hour later I finally hear Rania at the door.

❧

RANIA—

"Where is she?"

"The back bedroom."

"Has she been drinking?"

"Oh, yeah. She came in smelling like a tequila worm. Anyone else woulda been passed out by now but she's wide awake."

"What about drugs, did you ask Emilio?"

"I…"

"You didn't ask him? Jesus, Baca. Call him. Call him and find out."

And with that Baca goes for his phone and I walk down the hall to the guest room where I turn the knob and swing open the door. Dale is sitting up on the bed, her back against the white wall, the blanket wrapped around her. She looks up at me and offers me a lost smile.

"Rania," she says.

"Hi," I say, and I sweep down into her arms and give her what she needs most, a long long hug—the hug of a mother. Filled with love and all that is feminine. A hug from my heart and soul and I feel her soul accepting this love.

She asks, "Where's Emilio?"

"Forget Emilio. This is about you now. So talk to me."

"He brought me into this dark place. And it scared me."

"Tell me," I say. I release our hug and swing my legs up on the bed so we're sitting there, side by side, and I take her hand and say, "Tell me."

And she does, all of it. Ohio, then this experience tonight with Emilio, and I'm cursing him and loving him for this crazy effort he made with her, but they are both so far over their heads, and I'm worried for her because in work that goes this deep, you must come out the other side, you must break through or else there's damage. And now I'm worried that she was damaged here. But still, somehow, after all this, I still can't understand this person, Dale. I don't know how to read her.

"Tell me what is happening. You're in shock. Yes? You know that."

"Yeah. I guess."

"But how you got here, tell me. That is the key. You were riding him, your legs spread over him, his erection in your hands…"

"Mine. My erection."

"Your erection. And he was guiding you through all your masculine anger, hoping you could purge it, blow it out, and you did, you came, you released all that power, and that should have worked. Dale, that should have put you in a better place. But it didn't. Why? Tell me why."

Dale turns to me and says, "Am I a man?"

I smile. That's all I can do, I smile. A smile of relief, of love.

She asks again, "I mean somewhere deep inside me. Am I a man?"

I laugh and tell her, "No. No. You are not a man."

And that's all she needs. I see the relief spread across her face, through her entire body. One of the most unsettling of conditions, gender confusion. When we are not anchored in our masculine or feminine.

Dale is suddenly smiling and stroking my face. Then she laughs and says, "Yeah, well you're looking pretty good to me right now."

Then I realize that through all this trauma that she really is still quite drunk. Tequila. Oh, wonderful. The legal psychedelic.

"You must get some sleep," I say.

"Yes," she answers and I help her scoot under the covers and before I can even kiss her on the lips, she is asleep.

I kiss this sleeping girl on the lips.

Then I think of myself. Everything I've learned, everything I know, I am drawing on here. Here and now. With Dale, with this beautiful young woman who I have fallen so deeply in love with, who I will never be allowed to love. So I soak her in. I go to the deepest place I have in my soul and I turn it into a sponge and I soak her in.

Then I slip out and head back to the kitchen.

ॐ

EMILIO—

I know that Dale, she's okay. And yeah, so maybe I stretched it a bit there, but she needed that. She was asking for that. But I hate now how I got my Pops coming down on me, and then Rania to the rescue like some new age Malibu lifeguard. And right now they're probably up there banging each other, Rania and Pops. Maybe all three of them, who knows? And I'm the bad guy. I'm the bad guy? Fuck that shit. I'm going to bed.

BACA—

I see Rania coming at me and I say, "I called Emilio. No drugs. Just tequila."

"Good. Okay. So she'll be all right. No emergency room tonight. No ambulance."

"Good."

"Yeah."

We head to the bedroom and Rania crawls into bed with me and we make love. The old-fashioned way. Boy on top. Totally in awareness. Rania and me. It is sexy and spiritual, no one but us, slow and steady and building, the power, the speed, building the rhythm and I know her body so well, see the flush across her chest and breasts, and how suddenly she slows, almost freezes, goes into this pre-orgasm limbo, and me right there with her, so wanting to come, telling myself, don't try, don't try, so I don't try, and she's then coming in this strong, solid, womanly wave of orgasm, but me, I'm stuck. That place we get as we age, so close to orgasm but unable to plunge through. So I quiet myself and sigh and say, "Is it not strange that desire should so many years outlive performance?"

Rania snorts and says, "Baca, you can be many men, but Falstaff is not one of them. Fuck me now, baby. Fuck me, fuck me til you come."

And with that she reaches her hand across my ass and down to my base, and pushes there, that fleshy place between my asshole and my balls, pressing into my middle-aged prostate and I release like a motherfucker. I come and come and she comes and comes again.

And that is why it pays to make love with a woman of experience.

RANIA—

Some nights Shakespeare is to be left on the shelf. As we drift off to sleep, semi-spooning under the light down comforter, I feel him shift his hips, still awake. I whisper.

"I let go of her. Dale."

"Just like that?"

"Just like that. On the drive up here tonight, when I was so crazed with everything, I decided she's my daughter."

"She's your daughter."

"Yes."

"I like it," Baca says. "Sweet work."

"The power of suggestion."

"Makes things a lot cleaner."

"And now my new daughter is in love with your son."

"Oh, jeez," he says.

"Hey, if all this seems crazy, Baca, try reading the Greeks."

"I've read the Greeks. They're all nuts."

"They're meant to be together, you know. Dale and Emilio."

Baca agrees and we fall asleep.

ᘓ

EMILIO—

It's five a.m. I'm dreaming. I'm just a kid, a teenager—back at Mondo's with the wind howling, the waves crashing every which way, G. already out of the water, up the rocks, running for my dad, and me in the surf zone, fuck, I'm stuck here, I'm stuck, and it's cold and my leash broke but somehow I grabbed my board, but I don't know which way to turn now, the waves pounding me from everywhere and me, gasping for breath, knowing I'm losing it, and there's all sorts of shit in the water, everything in splinters—deck boards, pilings, furniture, I see a crib, a fucking crib and there's kelp all over me, pulling

175

my board away, and I look up and I see my Pops there, on the rocks, scrambling down, ripping off his clothes. For me. For me. I'm gasping, feeling water in my lungs now, I'm cold, so cold, and over my shoulder a wave that I know is gonna kill me, so I pull my knees up to my chest and wrap my arms around my knees, fourteen-years-old, man, fourteen, and I go under, and suddenly there she is—Dale, reaching out her hand.

❧

BACA—

It's Friday morning and everybody's feeling full of beans now, right? Me included. In a good way. And we all know, all of us, that there is no need for another word. All this psychological bullshit? Enough already.

I call Emilio and with my voice let him know that all is fine. He's going surfing. I decide to join him.

While Rania takes Dale shopping—plowing a trail through downtown Ojai, from the fancy boutiques to the thrift stores. It's very girlie. These two, hand in hand, arm in arm.

Rania and Dale, working that gold card, while Emilio, he and I are off to the ocean, off to the reef break at Solimar Beach and I'm with him out there and for him, today, it's not about tearing it up, it's about the groove. And that's what the ocean can do for you. That's how it can heal. When I see him in the waves sometimes I think he's a Selkie—the seal that turns into a man but must always return to the ocean, return to find himself, and I'm out there with him as he finds himself again.

We're having dinner together tonight. The four of us. It's been arranged. I'm cooking.

❧

DALE—

And I'm helping. I'm feeling so good. Manicure, pedicure, massage, all these new clothes, I'm feeling like such a fucking girl I could sell it, you know, package it up and say, hey— Girl for sale! Girl for sale! But mostly, I'm feeling the embrace of Rania and Baca. Like somehow all the energy changed overnight. And they're being so sweet to me. Just knowing Emilio is coming.

So it's crazy good right now, cooking dinner with Baca, Rania coming in and out, setting the table outside, arranging the chairs, lighting candles. All of us knowing that Emilio is coming. Emilio is coming, and I can see how Baca and Rania so much want this to work between him and me. They want me to love him.

So cool, that message they're making clear. But five minutes later I'm chopping peppers and I feel them, Rania and Baca, somehow doing that parent thing, reminding me without words, like I'm some little girl—remember, Dale—Emilio is the man.

Emilio is the man, Dale, and you are the woman. So act the woman and all will be fine.

And I'm like fine, okay, okay. I got it.

☙

EMILIO—

I had a nice talk with my Pops today. Coming in out of the water. I felt like he could really understand me. Understand where my soul was. And offering his help, offering to help me play it out. It was sweet. But then on the beach I started giving him some shit about this little paunch he's putting on, how he was getting all soft on everybody, and he's laughing, saying, you think I'm soft? You think I'm soft, and he's coming at me all crouched low and throwing all sorts of crazy kicks and punches and I'm dodging him in my wetsuit, dropping my board, then running away up the beach, yelling, Child abuse! Child abuse! Until I hear him grunt behind me and of course he pulled something, fucking old man, pulling up lame. But it was sweet. A nice time with my Pops.

∽

RANIA—

It will be a courtship, that's what we want. This dinner under the Ojai stars. A final blessing.

Emilio arrives in a white shirt and black pants. Sandals. He has slicked back his hair and put in a high clip, like a ninja almost, pulling his hair away from his forehead. He looks most handsome.

And Dale, she is beautiful. A simple pink t-shirt, a white skirt. No make-up, nothing. A pair of flip-flops I bought her with silver spangles on them.

Dale meets Emilio in the doorway and they kiss. Then Emilio sweeps into the kitchen and kisses me and kisses his father then kisses Dale again, and all with this crazy jabber of English and Spanish, Baca joining in, all platitudes, but offered in the most generous of ways, like a performance almost, something arch and quite European about it, or South American maybe, this faux flurry of words meant only for the sounds we create as I throw in some French and Arabic for good measure, a dance of notes played by four instruments as Dale finally joins in with some crazy rap, a freelance slew of rhymes conveying her happiness, and so it's quite the little quartet we've started here, yes? And this before dinner is even served.

⁓

BACA—

There is love in the air, that much is certain.

With Dale's help I have made a concoction of four simple dishes offered in four serving bowls—all to be smeared onto hot pita bread or a fresh leaf of Romaine bought by Rania at the farmer's market a very long five days ago. I have prepared tonight a curry paste of garbanzo beans. A mix of chopped raw ahi and ginger. Jerked chicken and peppers. And last, something that my grandmother taught me in Peru that I will not say what it is.

We sit down to eat and my hotshot young son says, "So Pops, this is it? Best you can do?"

And we laugh and I shush him with my middle finger as I walk back inside, returning then with a chilled bottle of a special Pinot Grigio that is both tasty with food like this and easy on the brain cells.

"This then for us. One glass each." I turn to the youngsters, "And for you two, after last night, you will thank me for allowing no more alcohol for you."

So I pour us each a glass and we raise our glasses in the evening light, in the candlelight, in the pink moment that just then hits, just right, the whole valley shuddering, and so we raise our glasses, looking into each others' eyes and we drink from the cup of life.

⁓

DALE—

They planned this whole thing. Keeping Emilio and me from being alone together. They turned it into this like family affair night, so what can I do but enjoy it? It's total perfect

179

harmony tonight, somehow everyone leaning forward and grabbing food, passing plates, and always, Emilio, across from me, as we all talk and laugh and listen, and catch each other's eyes. Emilio. Emilio.

But talk? Believe me, these three can talk.

They talk about money, God, Obama, monogamy, poly relationships, they talk about how difficult it is to keep the sex juice going in marriage, and then Baca goes on a riff about how it all works out better the better actor you are:

"Man, I refuse to be old. I don't have to be old. I can be my younger self. I can. Why not? And I'm not talking pretend, I'm talking feeling it. Method! Living like Al Pacino, man. Living like Dennis Hopper…!"

And finally it's Emilio who's laughing and shouting at him, "Enough! Enough of this!"

And then finally we all quiet down. It's time to go. But as we rise from the table, and all the crazy conversation is still swirling in my head, there is one thing that really sticks. One thing that Rania said:

"Love is like music. Every time you hear a song, you are in communion with the one who wrote it. And with everyone who ever heard it, sang it, played it and made love to it. It is the ripple of music. It is the ripple of love."

And I'm just lingering here in this daze when I see that Emilio is standing up and thanking Rania, and thanking Baca and kissing them each on the lips of course, then he reaches his hand across to me and says,

"Walk me out."

"Okay."

And we float through the house and out the front door to his van, and he's sweeping me into his arms and kissing me, then pulling back and staring into my eyes.

"I've been thinking about this. You're inside me now, a part of me, so I want to say something to you. I want you to be my girlfriend. For reals. And every way we can, we'll find a way to be with each other. And love each other. I want this, and…

"Emilio…"

"Ssshhh. Let me finish. So this is what I want, and I want you to spend the night thinking about it. Okay? Really. Think about it. Whether you want me or not."

He kisses me again. "Say, okay. That you'll seriously consider it."

"Okay."

"I'll be back tomorrow morning. And if you'll have me, I'm yours."

He kisses me, and he's gone.

I'm standing alone in Baca's driveway. Under the stars.

My tears are so filled with happiness I don't want to waste them. I want to catch them in my palms, put them in a jar, save them like fireflies. But I've changed, I'm letting go. So these tears, I let them drop from my cheeks and hit the still-warm concrete of the driveway. And that fast they're in the air. Evaporated. My tears drifting up into the night sky.

Where they belong.

৩

RANIA—

Baca and I make love again. Tantra-style. And what does that mean? I don't know. In touch, breathing in synchronization. With understanding and awareness. And love.

I want to be the first one awake, but Baca beats me to it. It's a special day. He and I have coffee. Some fruit. We wait. We talk. We are in agreement that this union of Emilio and Dale is blessed, although I maybe have a few more qualms.

We read the newspaper as Baca mutters, what is it about these kids, the most beautiful day of their lives and they sleep in…? We wait some more, until finally I am walking down the hall and knocking softly on Dale's door.

"Come in," she says.

I swing open the door and there she is, sitting up in bed, the most radiant smile on her face. So beautiful. So filled with love that even my most jealous heart can only give it up to her. To her and Emilio. To their love. Not mine. Theirs.

Suddenly she is anxious, "Do you think he'll come?"

"Yes," I answer. "Let's get you ready."

So I run a bath for her and hang around as she slips off her nightgown and steps into the hot steaming water and cleans herself with a bar of glycerine soap. Then I hand her a can of shaving cream and a razor and she shaves her legs. Then she feels under her arms and I say,

"Here, let me do this." So she sighs, and breathes deeply and raises her arms up against the blue tile behind her and her breasts rise just out of the water, her nipples barely exposed, and I splash hot water on her and apply the shaving cream and I shave under her arms.

"I love you, Rania," she says.

"I love you, Dale," I answer.

☙

BACA—

So my son better not fuck this up here or I'm gonna be really pissed off. Then I hear him coming through the front door. We hug and kiss and I look him straight in the eye.

"You're sure you know what you're doing here?"

"Not a clue, Pops."

"Good. The best place to start with a woman, no?"

We smile and laugh.

RANIA—

As Dale steps from the tub I dry her. This is my girl here. This is my soldier in the battle of love, and I anoint her with love and strength. The strength to hold her own and yet the love to surrender and share, and as I think these thoughts I'm sounding like a fruitcake to myself and I'm glad I'm not sharing them with her because she would say—What? Huh?

Then I notice her cootchie and the botched trim job and I say, "Dale, did you do this?"

"What? Yeah. You like it?"

"It looks like Edward Scissorhands or something, I don't know. Here, let me fix you."

"But he's here. Emilio. I heard his van."

"So what? Let him wait."

I tell Dale to climb up onto the counter and spread her legs and she does this as I find a comb and scissors and I pull over the stool and sit in front of her as the morning sunlight streams through the window onto her. Onto her sex, her love.

I lean in and go to work and in a few minutes she is beautifully trimmed, me snipping away in a trance of love and admiration, for this, the most beautiful vagina I have ever witnessed. The black of her hair, the pink of her labia, the deeper pink of her inner pussy. We are in a fog of love. Or me at least.

"May I kiss you here? A bon voyage?"

"Yes," she says.

So I lean forward, and I kiss her there.

A modest kiss, filled with love. But as the wet and scent of her hits my lips and nostrils I have to pull back. I'm afraid. Suddenly lost in the deep love and sex of her, the power of her sexuality and look at me, I'm on my knees in front of her. How did I get here? I hesitate knowing that to stay in integrity I cannot kiss her again.

But the devil in me makes me do it in fantasy, right there, as I'm kneeling in front of her—I am suddenly diving back in, as if stealing a deep kiss, Frenching her, parting her petals with my tongue and pushing my tongue inside her, knowing the full taste of her, then exiting, running my rigid tongue up over her clit, a flick, two, three, four, then taking a final bow with my lips simply kissing her lips, honoring her yoni, me soaking in every moment, every sensation, knowing that this is the first and last time that I'll ever have her.

A soft gentle kiss and a full heart of imagination. All I am to ever have.

I love her.

I love her.

But she loves Emilio.

ↄ

BACA—

Wait. Didn't you decide that from now on Dale was to be your daughter? Isn't that what you said?

RANIA—

A mother can't kiss her baby daughter's cootchie? Like in the old country, no?

BACA—

Dames.

ↄ

EMILIO—

It's Saturday morning and sure all this crazy shit has gone down, but I'm putting it behind me and so is everybody else.

184

DALE—

Rania has me stand in front of her and she puts this nice fragrant oil on me, on my neck, around my breasts, just a touch of it, then between my thighs. Then she finds this silk robe like some geisha thing or something and I'm like what? But when I put it on, I understand. A robe. A kimono. A cloth belt that she ties with a very elaborate knot. A knot someone once taught her.

The preparation of a woman in love.

BACA—

We have fun in the kitchen, Emilio and me, until the ladies finally make their entrance. Dale just blowing E. and me away in that kimono. Emilio so in love we can all feel his ache for her, and Dale so beautiful, so radiant, and of course me joking about how I could have played nine holes by now and Rania shushing me, then saying she's taking me to the beach and telling the kids that the studio is open, the studio is ready for you, then we're hugging and kissing goodbye and Emilio is suddenly looking deep into my eyes and saying, "Pops, go to Mondo's today."

"Yeah?"

"Yeah. It's breaking just the way you like it."

"Yeah?"

"Yeah. Word."

Then the two young lovers, Dale and Emilio, they take each other's hands and walk out the back door, heading for the studio.

Rania and I look at each other. "You good to go?" I ask her.

"Yes," she says, her eyes wet, her face filled with light and love.

❧

DALE—

Me and Emilio walking up through the pea gravel to the studio.

I'm wearing this crazy kimono robe thing and he's got on this blue t-shirt and these baggy shorts and flip-flops.

We're holding hands.

I'm letting go of a lot of stuff here. I am. On this walk up the pea gravel path.

I'm letting go of Ohio.

And as I do this, I'm thanking Emilio for that, remembering how I was such a shit to him, goin' all catatonic and shit like I did that night. What, two nights ago? Two nights. But what he did worked, you know? What he put me through. And having Baca and Rania back it up the way they did, it reassured me, you know? It made me feel that it worked, 'cause it did. It did.

So here I am.

I have this man who I believe is ready to love me. As I am ready to love him in return. Here I am, baby.

EMILIO—

Dale. I'm diving into her. I will act with love and awareness. With integrity.

❧

RANIA—

We take the Mercedes. Don't ask me why. I'm the one who can hardly stop crying. And Baca's spirit, so strong and silent alongside me, cruising down the 33, swinging onto the 101

North, me thinking we're heading for Rincon, the elbow, the safe place, off the highway, down the stairs, the perfect beach with the surfers and the Amtrak rolling through, overhead, just a glimpse and a rumble... but no, I know Baca wants something else, as if his hand is on the steering wheel, and I exit quickly at State Beaches and I'm swinging the Mercedes down under the overpass and suddenly it's a narrow strip of highway right there on the ocean, broken by a line of RVs then a line of houses, then a seawall and I say,

"Where?" But I know where. Mondo's.

☙

DALE—

We crunch up the path to the studio, Emilio and me, and it's not all solemn and stupid, right? 'Cause it's not like that, 'cause we both know, deep in our hearts, that this is real so we can let loose, have some fun with this, I mean, we're in this sacred zone okay? There's nothing hard about this. It's love. We know it's real and no one can fuck it up. Including us. Sorry, too late. And here's me, the old me, shouting out in my heart—"This love has left the station, motherfuckers!" But of course I don't shout it.

I'm supposed to be the girl here.

EMILIO—

I lead Dale up the path and across the deck. The studio doors are open, the mid-morning sun bouncing off the walls, and there is incense burning, and a single fat white candle has been lit alongside the red futon that is now stretched flat.

We kick off our shoes and I lead her inside, across the smooth bamboo floor. I suddenly grab her waist and turn her into my body and kiss her and say, "You are truly beautiful," and with these four simple words she becomes the girl she is. The woman she is.

She smiles at me, and as my hand reaches for the knot of her belt I lean forward and kiss her. I kiss her. I kiss her and kiss her until she knows it is me who is kissing her, it is Emilio, until she falls into me and kisses me back. Kisses me back until suddenly I step away from her and slip my left hand under the belt of her kimono, right over her center, her belly button, and we laugh because it's a bold move, but I know she's with me, so I've got hold of her belt and I tug her and walk her over to the edge of the futon with love and purpose and high arousal. I am offering her all of it, and she's receiving it. All of it.

DALE—

We're standing there face to face, our eyes so locked into each other, then he reaches again for the cloth belt to my kimono, and he slowly begins to untie the knot, but Rania tied this crazy intense knot, okay? Like a chastity belt of her mind or something, and it makes us both laugh, me and Emilio, because he has good strong fingers and determination and he will untie this knot of Rania's. Working it, probing it as he leans forward and touches his forehead to mine, and he lets it rest there, and I can feel him, the purity of his purpose through this touch, and then he pulls back and stares into my eyes, all the while still working this hard, intricate knot, and he begins talking:

"I want to make love to you softly and gently. With the lightest touch and the truest care. I know you now. And I want to make love to you."

I say nothing as I feel him getting that first link loosened and free. I feel his knuckles against my belly through the silk.

"We've spent days and nights. We've gone deep. Joys and sorrows and hurts… We slept together under the stars. We exposed ourselves in so many ways…"

And him talking on like this, in this hush voice thing, him so deep into my listening, and all the while him working the knot, working the knot of my kimono and our eyes so locked in. And now the knot is coming undone, I can feel the kimono begin to fall open as he kisses my lips, my neck and he continues,

"I love you, Dale and I want you to accept that love. I know you're ready. Everything you've been through, it's behind you now, and you're free to love, deeply, without guilt or reservation. To give and to receive. Receive me, will you? Say yes. Say yes."

"Yes."

I'm not in a trance. I'm hearing it and feeling it all, every touch, every word, all of these words like butterflies or something—fireflies—and they're fluttering over me and I'm feeling my entire body flush with his strong quiet masculinity. His strongest male. Emilio, he's bringing it as I look up into his eyes and smile and feel this crazy need to break the spell, just to catch my breath, and I say, "So you got your "A" game working here, huh, Mr. Poetry Man?"

Emilio smiles and says, "Ssshhh, girl, shush up. Feel my love for you."

And I feel how really he's being firm but gentle with me, us still standing there face to face, just so perfect as he slips me out of the kimono and lets it fall to the floor and he wraps his arms around me as he brings me down onto the futon, both of us, and it's like landing on a cloud, you know? Like with this guy's arms around me he can fly me anywhere. Anywhere. And after we land and bounce and settle in so gently, I lie there alongside him, face to face, and I smile at him even as I'm saying, hey, how come I'm the naked one here, but he's looking at me like, duh? So I laugh and kiss him and begin tugging at the steel button of his shorts.

I do this knowing that soon the energy will change and I will experience his hardest male.

I want that. I'm ready. Because Emilio, he's showed me his other side. Down the Sespe River. I understand him now. And I trust that today, this new day, that we are ready for each other. I want union with him, with Emilio.

EMILIO—

I want the same. Down on the futon, wrapping my arms around this beautiful naked girl as she tugs now at my zipper.

I offer and deliver a true kiss, a kiss that she can feel deep inside her, a kiss that makes her stop fumbling with my shorts as she returns this kiss and we kiss each other with deep love and awareness. I finally lift my lips from hers, and we lock eyes.

"Are you warm enough?" I ask.

We're spread out on the red futon with the sun pouring in and the heat just flowing through, flowing through the studio. Flowing through our bodies.

"Oh yeah," she says.

"Then let me get to know you."

DALE—

Oh, God. Emilio, he owns me. Right now, he owns me and that little part of me that's still resisting, I'm saying, girl, get over it. Because if there is ever a man who can love me, understand me, own me, and give it up to me, it is this man. It is Emilio.

☙

RANIA—

Mondo's is quiet, an in between tide, easy sets of gentle waves rolling in. There's a nice mix of parents and kids out, getting a taste, a cold wet salt taste of it, longboards, foam boards, fun boards, the water still chilly, everybody in black wetsuits.

I struggle down the rocks, reaching for Baca's hand, and it's strong and steady. We finally reach the sand. We remembered to bring nothing, no towels, no beach chairs, no umbrella, but it is now late morning and the sun is burning off the mist over the quiet ocean and we bask in its warmth. I lean over. Against his shoulder. Always there for me. Always. No matter why or what or where. That shoulder, always there for me.

છ

EMILIO—

I explore the entire garden of Dale's body. All the delights and most of the secrets, my fingers and lips and tongue everywhere on her. Moving alongside her, over her, in the warm morning sun, up and down the length of her body. I'm not forcing issues here, I'm not looking for any more knots to untie. I just want to know every inch of her.

I have deliberately stayed away from her yoni, the sum of her sex. I feel its heat and power and love and I let it simmer there, between her thighs, her three closest chakras pulsing with heat and light and love. Her yoni, present there like an icon. A goddess. Stewing with power and love and lust.

I decide to lighten the mood and I blow a wet kiss on the skin of her belly, then find myself, my face, my cheek, lying across the angle of her pelvis, from hip bone to her navel, my head resting here, my hair falling down over her skin, her fingers in my hair, me taking in the feel and scent of her, as I look down and across, the pulsating close-up visual of her as this beautiful flesh of hers catches the morning light and from my point of view, up close, my eyes level with the skin of her, I see the tiny hairs rise, the tiniest of hairs, around her perfect navel, as if each wants a voice this morning, each tiny little goose pimple of pleasure has a song to sing in the symphony of her body.

191

DALE—

Man, I am fucking to the moon here. I'm so wet and horny I'm thinking where else is this guy gonna take me before I get where I want to be?

Give it to me already! Hey, E., bring it, bring that big hard dick of yours and let's rock this thing already, but of course he's gonna do it his way and I tell myself to slow down, because for the first time in my life I am with an enlightened male, a man in total touch. So he'll do it his way, and I gotta admit that it's him who's created this energy field, it's him who's made this whole thing happen—where I'm going, where he's taking me. Okay then, I'm there. I'm there. I'm there with him.

∾

RANIA—

We dig our toes into the sand. Baca and me. My eyes fill with tears.

"Quit bawling, will ya?" he says and I do.

"You know what we've got here, right?" he says. "With her. Dale."

"What?"

"She's gonna turn into some crazy sexual evangelist."

"What? What are you talking about?"

∾

EMILIO—

I've touched every nerve in Dale's body, I have moved slowly, responding to her breathing at every step, getting her breath and my breath working together as I touch and kiss and tongue my way up and down this long delicious body of hers.

192

And now, finally, I bring my mouth down between her thighs. I do it with purpose, no hesitation. My mouth finds her yoni and I simply express my love for her sex with the deepest, fullest kiss any yoni can ever receive, and it is not about sex, it is not about orgasm, it is not about titillation or foreplay, it is simply and deeply my full-on love and appreciation for her, me kissing her pussy, staying with it, kissing and probing with my tongue and feeling her response in the subtle shifts of her hips, the shifts that sends her back to my lips, my tongue, me knowing that we are in sync with this kiss. This kiss of ours. My mouth to her pussy.

DALE—
This feels really really good.

I feel like I have this amazing Greek god down between my legs, like Socrates or something, and he knows exactly what he's doing. His father taught him well. With every touch of his tongue, every probe of his fingers, I grow more aroused, like a chess game almost, he keeps moving the pieces forward, I don't know, but he's on this slow build deal here, he's not gonna rush. Building this deep passionate love, building this energy field that is surrounding us, flooding our bodies. I mean I am absolutely buzzing here. But now suddenly he's backing off a bit, slowing me down again, his head still down between my open thighs, looking up at me, grinning, laughing almost, as I feel a single finger enter my vagina and find what it's looking for, just inside, curling up, pushing up into this wet sponge of flesh I never knew existed.

Until Ojai.

I gasp. I moan. I suck a breath then find some rhythm to my breathing. I am highly aroused now. Highly aroused. Then, when his wet tongue is there again, against my clit, on my clit, teasing my clit, sliding up one side then down the other, as his finger works some magic inside me, his tongue then zeroing in on me, his tongue strong and wet, working back the hood of my clit, finding it then, tonguing me, tonguing me with a long easy 7-11 Slurpie kind of tongue all hot and cold and red and blue and hard and soft and icy on me and I'm like, Whew, I'm running it, I'm feeling it, I don't know but it gets me laughing, because I know he's gonna back off again. No early climax for this little missy. Emilio has more for me. Oh, God. Oh, God.

ↄ

BACA—

We stare out at the ocean. The ocean is all shimmer blue, the beach with that dreamy, slow-down feeling—kids' voices, white foam, warm sand, the surf rumbling in, wave after wave after wave. Very spiritual stuff.

"Think he got her off yet?" I say.

"Baca!"

"What? That is the goal, no?"

"I'd like to think love has a place in there too."

"Of course, but I'm telling you, that girl, once she gets a real taste of it. Finally breaking through… *le convertimos en un evangelista sexual.*"

"No way," says Rania. "She's a painter."

ↄ

DALE—

When Emilio raises his mouth away from my pussy I cry out in frustration. I moan at him. My eyes still fluttering as my pussy shudders and pulses. I'm feeling the juices flowing, my clit as hard as it's ever been. He's already brought me to a place I've never been. Already. I open my eyes to this body of his moving back up on me, Emilio, smiling, rising up onto his knees on the red futon as he pulls his blue shirt up off over

194

his head, and I'm realizing, oh, God, he's not even naked yet, I've been so lost, so lost with his mouth on me, and now I'm wanting to make it right, to return the favor, but instead he's shushing me, maintaining control, smiling, rolling away as he pulls his shorts off down the long length of his legs, and I'm so flushed with sex I'm fucking dying here, okay? Enough of this new age stuff, I want him now, I want him because I can already feel him rushing through my whole body even though he's rolled away, because I know he's there, I feel him, he's there and he's hard. He's hard for me and tender for me, he loves me, he loves me and I want him in me.

I want him in me.

"Emilio."

He smiles. "Hey. Are you good with this?"

"Yes."

"I'm clean you know. Tested. You?"

"Yeah," I say. "But no babies here. Right? No babies."

"No babies."

"Cause I'm feeling like, we could make a baby just by breathing right now. Just by breathing."

"No babies. Guaranteed."

And so I'm ready for him. Ready to give it up to this beautiful, soulful, magnificent man.

And that's what I do. As I drop my head back on the red futon in the warm morning light. As I spread my arms and legs to him. Swell my breasts and belly upward at him. Then sneak a peek as he kneels before me, his erection filled with purpose. He leans forward and presses the length of his body down onto mine, forcing my thighs further apart, and I'm thinking, he'll go slow here, right? He'll be gentle, but I feel suddenly his true masculine energy, his true purpose, and he is not so gentle as he first begins to enter me, and I'm adjusting to that, and I know I'm wet enough, wetter than wet, as I feel his strong chest pressing down onto me, his hands pinning my wrists to the futon, and it's forceful, but I feel an understanding there, in his every action, in the force, the masculine urge, but also in the tenderness, as he holds me down, holds me open, so open.

But still a last part of me is still fighting it, even with his hard penis just inside me now, making his way inside me.

Until I finally surrender.

Because there is no resisting him. Emilio. As his second strong thrust plunges deeper into me, into my most precious place, I suddenly understand that this man, this man Emilio, he truly knows me as a woman. Maybe I'm only twenty-three, but I'm a woman, I have had my share of lovers in this crazy life, and that is fine by him, and that is how he is treating me, how he is entering me, not like I'm some virgin, but matching his powerful masculine spirit to my powerful feminine and this now is all right by me.

Emilio has entered me knowing that I can handle his entrance. And I do.

I am not some little girl. I am not a princess. I'm not somebody's little sweet pea. I am a woman.

And then we rock it.

I spread my legs farther apart, arching my back, raising my hips, meeting him. His every thrust deeper and deeper into me, long and slow at first, my pussy dripping wet, slimy wet, encouraging him to continue, and he does, long and slow, these strokes that I urge along, urging him along because I am wanting speed, speed now, bring it faster, but Emilio, he's long and slow, deep and full until finally I understand and I get control of my breathing as he lowers his lips to kiss me, and we are finally in true sync here.

EMILIO—

I know she is coming before she does. Through every pore of her skin she is coming. As I continue thrusting into her, with rhythm and purpose and the two of us in the perfect glide

196

now between us, where we are not so much clashing as rolling with each thrust, and me hearing her now, through her breath, her moans, that her clit is wanting for more, more than just the rhythm of my pelvic bone upon it, so I stick my thumb in Dale's mouth and I say, lick it, make it wet, and she does and I move my hand down towards her crotch, our bellies smacking against each other as I keep plunging into her. Thrusting. Plunging as she opens herself up to me even more, her body, her soul, this powerful soul of hers and she's feeling this now, as the beautiful woman she is, because this is with love now, with love and purpose, as she squirms underneath me, my manhood deep inside her, as my hand, my wet thumb fights for the space to reach her.

DALE—

I'm delirious, I'm feeling absolutely safe and free and so deeply in love and so sexual. For the first time. For the first time in my life. I am feeling the power of the feminine. That I can meet this man on equal terms. That I don't have to get all twisted. Because of love, and the balance, the Yin and Yang. The flow of energy, I'm understanding, I'm feeling it. It is all one to me. All one.

And now I feel the touch of his wet thumb on my clit, his strong hand wedged in between our bellies, finding me, stroking, in perfect rhythm. In perfect rhythm. As he continues to fuck me, but now his thumb on my clit, stroking it, stroking it, knowing just what a woman needs, to keep the rhythm, to stay with it, there's no breaking it now, it just keeps moving and moving, faster and faster in response to my breaths growing deeper and louder and faster, my chest heaving now, my beautiful titties smashing into his hard chest, he knows, Emilio, he knows, he knows what I need. He knows how to get me off and now I'm smiling, I'm smiling because I'm there, I'm already there, and yeah it's under his thumb with his dick in my cunt, but it's with love and conviction and I am a totally willing participant and I approve this message.

I come.

For the first time in my life, I come. Like "Houston, we have the solution!" I come in this series of hot, pulsing waves that shudder up and down my body—it's chakra demolition derby baby, that's what I'm talking about, everywhere, every pore, every fucking capillary of my body, pulsing with orgasm as I come in wave after wave, hot juice flowing out of my cooch, and I feel Emilio orgasming with me, him doing that shuddering spasm thing that men do, his ass so tight and hard, and for a second I'm afraid he's forgetting that I'm fertile, no babies here, no babies, but then I feel his hard dick jerk out of my twat just in time, like the master of manhood that he is, and his big cylinder of love splatting flat and hard down onto my belly, and I feel his hot cum squirting out, filling my navel, dripping down my flanks and it feels oh so good to me. So filled with light and love. Freedom from the past. As I shudder and spasm beneath him, wave after wave of sex and love washing through my body, consuming me, with this strong, beautiful man on top of me, the splash of his cum against our bellies.

And then our breathing finally quiets, our bodies slowly fading, then shuddering, relaxing, then shuddering again in a last tremor of orgasm. And now that I've made it, now that I am here I'm so fucking glad for this. For all of it, laughing, shouting at Emilio.

"I love you! I fucking love you, Emilio!"

And I cling to him, we cling to each other, and I'm thinking how I owe Rania so much, for bringing me here, for making this possible. I cling to Emilio, cling with love and hope. Love and happiness.

❧

RANIA—

We're lying back in the warm sand now, Baca and me. A slow warm pulse has been building in my body, I felt it spreading out from my between my legs, so I had to lie back, close my eyes. "They did it!" I shout out. "She came!" I look over at Baca. He's flushed. Breathing deeply.

"I know," he says. "I felt the earth shake."

"Oh, bullshit," I say, laughing.

"Really. You didn't feel that?"

"It was probably your hemorrhoids."

❧

DALE—

I'm flat naked on the red futon, exhausted with love and orgasm, my body still shuddering, my heart and soul filled with the most sensational fullness. Like a full moon. Like the ocean. Emilio slowly raises his body off of mine, his cum gone sticky, his eyes clear and blue.

"I love you, Dale."

"I love you, Emilio."

He rolls off and lies down beside me. We hold hands and breathe deeply. I love this about Emilio. How he can go so quiet and how nice it is. After a while I'm suddenly overcome with this clarity of purpose. Like I know now what I have to do. I'm thinking of all those girls out there. All those women who've been hurt, pushed down, shoved around. Used, abused. And how they turn it on themselves. Like I did. But now I see how there's a way out. They've showed it to me. Rania, Baca, Emilio—they've shown me the way through. And now I'm like, hey, it's time to pay it forward, right? It's what I've gotta do now. So many girls just like me...

RANIA -

"I told you," says Baca.

"Merde," I reply.

"Cry havoc. Let slip the dogs of war."

"And of love."

"Yeah, that too."

THE END